DON'T FORGET TO DREAM!

OUTBACK CHRONICLES

R.L. PRIOR

First published 2024 by R.L. Prior

Produced by Independent Ink
independentink.com.au

Cover design by Catucci Design
Edited by Michelle Perry
Internal design by Independent Ink
Typeset in 12/17 pt Adobe Garamond Pro by Post Pre-press Group, Brisbane

Cover image credits
iStock-508856988.jpg
iStock-1353543958.jpg
iStock-1153170151.jpg
iStock-504035609.jpg
iStock-537645170.jpg
iStock-1289668697.jpg
iStock-1131571416.jpg

Internal image credits:
Page i – Shed drawn by Toby Prior
Page 97 – Jessie sketch by Toby Prior
Page 125 – Handwritten sheet music by Adam Connelly

ISBN 978-1-7637059-0-6 (Paperback)
ISBN 978-1-7637059-1-3 (epub)
ISBN 978-1-7637059-2-0 (Kindle)

This book is
dedicated to my children,
Casimir & Scarlett,

AND TO ALL THE VETERANS.
If you cross paths with Death
and your eyes draw to lock.
Tip your cap, grit your teeth,
You're not done here yet.

Acknowledgments

I thank my parents Larry and Rhonda Prior, and brother Toby Prior for their continuing support and encouragement in all my endeavors. Thanks to my former ADF colleagues for always keeping me in check and willing me to never yield, no matter how my wild idea was. To my family and friends, who underpin my life in ways that they may not even realise, thank you for always being there no matter the length of time that passes between greetings. Thank you to my editor Michelle Perry for her guidance and advice throughout writing stages of this book and Ann Dettori and her team at Independent Ink for making this book come to life, I couldn't have done it without you.

DON'T FORGET TO DREAM!

NOTES FOR THE READER

It needs to be stated that the accents an Australian or 'Aussie' person incorporates into their English can easily get lost in the dialogue when words are placed onto paper.

When you see this underline; __ under an italicised letter(s) it means you must raise the pitch, sometimes up to a perfect 5th! (i.e., C to G).

Depending on how exited a person is …

This could also be used with uncertainty when asking a question: 'Do you under_stand_?'

And if someone (mostly adolescent) is trying to prove a point or deliver an ultimatum, the last letter of a word may be delivered with exertion, resulting in an extra syllable, such as: 'No, Dad-Dah! I will not be doing tha-Ta!'

Pronunciation of letters seems to change with country casualness; exchanging the T for D is common practice: 'That'll be right!' becomes *'Thad'll be right!'*

The same effect can be done with a name such as Harveston, which becomes *Harvesdon.*

Also of interest: twenty-two song references are scattered throughout this book, adding to its playlist. Some are obvious, and some are hidden. You can turn to the final page (at risk of spoilers) and refer to the song list. Or, if you can wait until the end, you can crosscheck each page to see how many you found.

PROLOGUE

December 2023

'Why do we have to visit Grandad every week, Mum?' Atticus implored his mother as they walked up the bland-white hallway of the Royal Brisbane Hospital, past the largely framed painting of a billabong bush landscape. Atticus tried to read the name of the artist's signature as he followed his mother, who walked side by side, holding his younger sister's – Maggie's – hand.

Just before they turned left to enter the B wing, his mother replied, 'I told you already, Atti, it's important for you to chat to your grandad. He has some good stories to tell, and it will be great for him to keep sharing them with you.'

Atticus nodded, knowing full well that while he loved his grandad, the stories he had already heard usually were on repeat. So, he decided to push for new ones he hadn't heard before.

When they entered his grandad's room, Atticus couldn't help but smile brightly when he saw him sitting up straight in his hospital bed, looking eagerly at their arrival. His face crinkled with the signs of a 'foul-weathered life', but the cheer that exuded from his eyes always delighted Atticus.

His mother headed quickly over towards the bed and started fluffing the pillows and brushing off the bedsheet before asking, 'How are you holding up, Dad? Are you havin' a good time?

Fred wasn't her father, but Julie had affectionately referred to him as 'Dad' since before her children were born.

A nurse entered the room and began to scrub the floor around the bed next door.

Fred glanced at Julie, smiled and replied, 'Can't complain, and besides, no one will listen anyway, right?' He then called to the nurse, 'You're worth more than the nickel and dime you get paid, love.'

The nurse looked to be in her 50s, and her head bobbed above the bed as she replied to him, 'Oh, you're too kind, Mr Fine.'

Julie then asked her son, 'Atticus, can you wait with Grandad while Maggie and I go to the farm?'

Fred looked at her with surprise and sharply questioned, 'What farm? You just got here.'

Julie smiled. 'Just the farm café downstairs, Dad. Do you want anything?'

'No, I'm okay, Julz,' Fred replied, reaching over to pull the chair next to his bed closer towards him, motioning with his arms to Atticus to come take a seat.

But Atticus stood still.

Julie took Maggie's hand, and as they walked out the room, Fred said, 'Oh, actually, could you get us a notepad and pen, please. I've been having ideas, but not being able to write them down is driving me insane.' He looked at Atticus and then down at the seat, as if he was trying to get Atticus to read his mind, but Atticus didn't budge. 'Do you like snakes, Atti?' he asked.

'No, Grandad!' Atticus replied sharply.

'Yes … well, the staff reckon they saw a red-bellied black snake slithering around the floor here this morning, so you'd better take a seat to be safe.'

With one eyebrow raised, the nurse looked unapprovingly at Fred.

Atticus quickly jumped up on the seat and got comfortable. He then watched as the nurse left, before asking, 'Hey, Grandad …'

'Yes, my boy.'

Curiosity had been itching Atticus since he had taken part in his school's Anzac Day march again this year; he was almost twelve years old, and in grade six. 'What was it like back in the olden days, like after the war?'

Fred rubbed his chin as he looked over at him.

'Has your father ever told you about how we got into the motel business?'

'No, I don't think so,' replied Atticus, inching his way further towards his grandad.

'And did he ever tell you about a group called the Jerky Boys?'

Atticus laughed. 'What is a "Jerky boy"?' he asked with humorous wonder.

Fred's smile showed symmetrical creases along the inside cheek line, and the divot in his chin stretched tight. And then with an excited tone, Fred whispered, 'Well, my boy, do I have some stories for you!'

Atticus looked at the right side of Fred's stomach, where a scar curled around like a hooked knife up to his rib cage. 'How did you get that scar, Grandad? Was it in Vietnam?'

Fred looked up at the clock. 'Right, we don't have time for that story, but this one I'm about to tell you stays between you and me, got it?' He winked at Atticus. Fred then continued, 'Back in Harves*don*, the Jerky Boys had been playing tricks and getting up to no good.' Fred looked out the window; it let light in, but the view was only of white painted brickwork. He then looked back at Atticus. 'Well, it was the same day of old bushman Uncle Jack's funeral. He was about to do something terrible for Harves*don*, with that bloody coal mine company, so, as macabre as it is to say, it worked out well that he up and died when he did.'

Atticus eyeballed the fruit box apple juice on the bedside table, but paused, not wanting to interrupt his grandad by asking for it.

Fred continued, 'Anyway, that's another story, which we'll get to another day.' He stopped looking out the window and peered at his grandson, who was still eyeing off the apple juice. 'Want a popper juice, boy?'

'Why is it called a "popper"?' Atticus asked, gratefully taking the drink and punching a hole in the top of the box with the straw.

'You can ask your father when you get home ... now where was I ...'

Atticus took a big draw on the popper straw and looked up at his grandad. 'Something about the Jerky Boys.'

Fred's eyes suddenly widened. 'That's right ... the story goes that they were coming home from a party in a souped-up Holden – most likely, they'd been causing mischief, when all of a sudden ...'

Chapter One

WATCH OUT FOR THAT COW

1 August 1981

The target was always one hundred 'miles per hour' in the town of Harveston, until the metric system was introduced into new car models in 1974. Seven years later, Mick and his mates all received their learners driving licence at high school and borrowed their parents' cars to gain experience on the road.

However, they continued to refer to the imperial units, as did their parents.

The roads driven in their area out west were still made of dirt, long and windy with sudden 'ups-and-downs' over wooden creek bridges, which each had a unique rattle and clang. The long stretch from the west going east into town comprised of a gradual incline of close to eight hundred metres at the peak, with a giant drop directly after the top, followed by another five hundred-metre straight and two sets of ups-and-downs. Two small, pointed hills either side of the ups-and-downs resembled pimples, like the ones on Spud Moreton's face.

On this Saturday morning, Timmo was sitting in the front passenger seat, while Spud was driving. Mick was in the back left seat, and Biddy was in the back right – no seat belts were available in the back seats of the lightly dusted blood-orange HT Holden Monaro Coupe.

Mick watched Percy's front block pass by; it was the one with thick, rugged bush, short shrubbery, and with prickly pears peppered among it. Percy, the old jackaroo who owned the property, left the front block untouched, for privacy, while the back blocks were cleared for grazing beef cattle grasslands.

On the opposite side, out Biddy's window, the land had every tree cleared with burnt dry grass still smoking. The remnants of a fire had not long gone out. For a second, Biddy thought of his brother, Darcy, and he scrunched up his eyes and nose in pain, trying his hardest to push the memory of the house fire back into its corner. He had to look away and met Mick's eyes; both then realised that Spud was readying to attempt the speed target on the stretch coming into town.

There was a cassette tape in the car stereo, the first release of a new band called Australian Crawl, and Spud loved them. All four boys would get together at either of their houses every Sunday night to watch *Countdown* and see the latest bands play along with 'Molly's Melodrama'. They'd all wait in anticipation each week to see what antics Molly would have up his sleeve.

Spud stared straight into the road ahead, and without diverting his eyes, he pushed the tape into play, and the spool began to spin. He then turned up the volume louder. The song 'The Boys Light Up' started to blare from the six-inch round door speakers. Spud looked at the others. The harmonica started humming, and when the cowbell kicked in, Spud spat his strawberry gum out the window and got a crazed look in his eyes – the one he only ever got when things were about to become unhinged. With excitement lacing his voice, Spud yelled, 'Let's light 'm up, aye, boys!'

Spud was one year older than the other three, already having his full licence and buying his first car with his hard-earned cash at the age of sixteen. It sat in the garage for a year, and Spud continued working in his dad's butcher shop after school and as a floor boy on the kill floor during Christmas holidays at the abattoir in the neighbouring town. Even as a teenager, he was known around Harveston for a strong work ethic.

The car stopped still at the designated starting point of the stretch as Spud tried to measure his madness. All the boys were still recovering from last night's shenanigans at the rodeo.

'I'm not sure I'm up for this, Sp*ud*,' Biddy mumbled from the back.

Mick took a sip from his stubby and replied, 'Let's see what this girl can do.'

All boys then gripped the 'suicide handle' above their heads tightly, with the other hand holding a firmer grip onto their yellow-labelled brown stubbies.

'*headin' for my mountain home … where all the ladies' names are Joan*,' Spud sang as his left foot pushed on the brake, and his right foot on the accelerator.

Biddy yelled a cheeky dig over the top of the revving engine, 'Your mum's name is Joan, aye, Mick?'

'Biddy, shut ya mouth,' Spud replied, his orange beast beginning to gradually rev harder as the tacho climbed higher, almost to redline. 'You ready, boys?' he called, but before a response could be returned, he let go of the brake pedal. The V8 308-engine roared, and they all flew back into their seats as the car lurched from the starting point, going faster and faster up the stretch, running parallel with barbed-wire fences.

They raced along the red dirt road, and as they approached the peak, large plumes of rusty-coloured dust bellowed in the car's wake, and the sound of stones hitting the underbody of the car were like hail on a tin roof.

With the song's chorus approaching, Mick tried to get a glimpse of the speedo. He could see it climbing towards the target, but it was not quite going to reach one hundred by the peak of the hill. The car wheels left the earth momentarily as they sailed over the top at high speed then plunged down the other side, just as the song lyrics started singing '*oh no-no-no-no-no*'.

Biddy lost his tallie when his body drifted somewhat weightless mid-flight, and Timmo's hat somehow got knocked off, ending up in the back seat.

Mick looked across and gave a nervous laugh while yelling, 'Bloody Jeezus, Spud-Da!'

Spud was focused hard on the road.

Timmo hung on as-tight-as-he-could to the handle; it was moments like this he wished for his missing fingers to somehow return. His right arm was braced with his hand pushed hard against the black vinyl dash like an expected stern co-pilot would if a plane was coming in for an emergency landing.

The car sped down the hill towards the ups-and-downs, and Spud was glad the council had recently graded the road's surface.

The boys thought the worst had been and gone, unaware of what lay waiting ahead.

Quickly, they whizzed over the two quick hills, beer flying through the air and their bodies losing gravity on each peak in time as the song began to crescendo.

At the bottom of the second hill, Mick yelled out to Spud, 'Watch out for that COW!'

The breaks were pumped hard, and Spud Moreton

even pulled the hand break as the car skidded, sliding slowly into the unforeseen, white-speckled Brahman cow that was casually crossing the road.

Timmo's 'Wilhelm' scream may have been the last thing the bovine heard; not having a second to turn its head to see what was coming, and on impact, the cow rolled up and over the front end of the orange Monaro, smashing the windscreen and leaving a trail of muck on the glass along the way.

Spud's car landed off to the side of the road, nose down into the steep gutter, narrowly avoiding a thick grey iron-bark tree to the left and a telephone pole to the right.

The four boys looked at each other; the music was somehow still blaring from the speakers.

Spud piped up, 'Everyone ok_ay_?'

It felt like ten seconds of waiting before Biddy replied, 'Yes, you mad bastard. I think you sure fucked that cow though.'

Timmo wiped the beer from his forehead and was quick to quip, 'Wasn't the first and won't be the last, aye, Spud.' He laughed.

Spud would usually have something to rebut; however, nothing came to mind this time as he paused in slight shock.

Mick piped up, 'Guys, we should get-ouda here. Good chance that's one of Percy's mob, and he'll string us up if he finds out. Let's head up over those hills and circle around them to get home.'

Timmo added, 'Don't worry, Spud, let's grab my dad's *new* Land Cruiser and snig chain, then hide the car under his workshop floor … What do ya think?'

They jumped out to assess the damage to the car and cow.

Mick examined the cow and stated, 'I think she's in calf!'

'Shit, Spud-Dah! Poor girl, eh man … we gotta get a move on.'

Spud was quiet as they walked in single file, thankful nobody was hurt. Then he stopped short, turned around and ran back to the car.

'What are you doing now?' Timmo grumbled.

Spud reached through the driver side door window, leant in with his brown leather Blundstone boots dangling out, and grabbed the cassette tape before turning around to catch up with the others, proclaiming, 'This one is too good to leave behind.'

Only twenty-four hours earlier, the boys had met at the footy oval to carpool together in Spud's car, driving one hour west towards a bush rodeo meet, planning to camp there overnight. Mick pinched half-a-dozen brown tallie bottles from his dad: Colin's home-brew collection. Biddy supplied the esky, which sat in between the boys in the back seat, and it was stocked with ice and a brown bottle of rum, and Timmo took 'some kind of sweet American bourbon' from his parents' liquor cabinet.

Spud was driving, so intended not to drink, and brought only a kilo of his dad's jerky from his butcher shop to snack on and a few bottles of sarsaparilla, which the other boys could use as mixers in their spirits.

It was always a wild night whenever they got together and carried on. Their stories would be told the following week at school, with most kids just waiting in anticipation to hear of the crazy tales of excitement and mischief-making.

Seeing as Spud had his licence and a car, he had become the main portal to the outside world. This opened the gates to newfound trouble in areas they had not been able to access at an earlier age when handcuffed to their parents' side.

The boys now looked back at the blood-orange Monaro as they walked up around the mountain.

'You're not having much luck with cars this year, are you, Spud,' stated Timmo.

Seeing it with steam spewing out of the crushed-up bonnet only worsened their deflated mood, or maybe that was the alcohol from last night? Either way, they weren't scared of anything until they saw the procession heading towards the scene of the crash, slowing down to a stop.

Timmo made the unnecessary comment, 'Shit, boys! I think we might be in some trouble now.'

His statement needed no response. The boys just hid behind one of the large grey stone pillar boulders and peered around both sides to see what was going to happen next.

Mick recognised Fred Fine. 'That's Mr Fine, he's mates with Johno. Ahhh, shit. The funeral was today!'

They watched Fred hop out from his car, which was third behind the lead car. He walked over to the cow laying on its side in the middle of the road. Fred had dark tan-leathered skin from years in the sun and usually wore a brown Akubra hat, which sat just above and covered his furrowed brow, but his chiselled jawline was still notice-able from that distance.

Spud piped up, 'What the bloody hell are they gunna do? Surely, there's enough room for them to drive around the poor girl.'

The wind picked up from the west, blowing the cumulus clouds in front of the sun. The boys had shade for a moment, no need to squint, as they watched on in the same way a crow observed a picnic in the park, waiting for people to clear out. Their jaws began to drop when they saw what was unfolding in front of them.

Biddy randomly whispered, with a crackly voice, 'Gee, Mick, those beers you brought along last night tasted sour, and I think some of them had lumps in them.'

Mick decided to tell them, 'Yeah … well, I think they had another couple of weeks fermentation left until they were ready'.

Timmo held his stomach with both hands and said, 'No wonder my guts feel crook.'

'I thought it was worth trying them to see what they were like … lesson learnt,' Mick admitted.

The boys stood still, looking down on the gathering that had formed around the cow, unable to make sense of what was happening. However, from behind the rock, they could see Fred Fine sitting behind the cow.

Five minutes, or so it seemed, went by, and they saw a calf pulled from its mother, and Fred trying to help it stand on its feet.

'Holy crap,' Mick said.

The next minute, Percy walked over. He aimed his rifle at the cow's head, and a shot rang out that echoed through the hills.

Spud declared, 'Jeezus, shit! This party's over, boys, we better move it and try to get the Land Cruiser before they're done out at the cemetery and come back in for the wake.'

With a noticeable increase of pace, once again in single file, the four boys started off along the well-trodden dirt cattle track cut into the hillside to carry on as planned.

Timmo, at the tail-end, yelled, 'Hey, Spud, you ever try putting that song on while I'm in the car and you'll be Aussie crawling the entire way home.'

Chapter Two

FRED FINE

January 1981

Johno looked at Fred as they sat on the park bench having just picked up their breakfast pies from Arthur's Bakery.

'I can't do this anymore, Johno,' Fred exclaimed, rolling his eyes and sighing.

'What, the pie? You could get a sausage roll next time, Fred?'

'No, I mean this life, for Chrissake, it's … I feel like I'm drowning. Every night, we drink and drink until one of us passes out … or Reg gives us the boot.'

'Yeah …'

'I mean, really, this has been going on for years since I got back. Either I'll drink myself to death or be run over by a road train one night staggering home from the pub, don't you think?'

A magpie swooped in and landed on the grass under

the lilli pilli tree behind them. It started to sing its morning tune as if trying to get their attention.

Johno watched the bird for a moment while it dug its beak into the grass. His memory allowed him to almost taste the slightly tart qualities of the purple lilli pilli fruit they once picked sitting under the bush as kids. He gave time before he spoke, sensing the weight of the topic and knowing this was a pivotal moment for Fred. 'Donald, a dolphin, is sick … He's been feeling down and not really enjoying life, ya know?' he remarked. 'He goes to the doctor and says, "Doc, I'm not sure what to do anymore. I've tried everything, and I still feel like I'm constantly seasick." Well, the doctor leans forward and places Donald's flipper near his blow hole and states, "Donald, you need to find your *porpoise* in life."'

Fred scoffed with a puff ball of air sound as pastry flies from his mouth. 'Jeezus, Johno, you're probably right. But I'm thinking about getting a dog … at least it won't say stupid things to me like you.'

Johno sniggered. 'Well, I'm thinking about getting the fire pit going and doing a meal in the camp oven tonight. Do you want to come over?'

'Sounds good, Johno, I'll pop over after work,' Fred replied with a glint in his eye. While Johno's jokes never consistently hit the target and often hit too close to home, Fred knew he could always count on Johno. He laughed to himself thinking about the time 'drunk Johno' told him 'ya know, Fred (hiccup), if you ever needed someone killed, I'd kill for you, mate.' Fred couldn't tell if Johno was serious or not, but the statement was said with a slow drawl, and the hiccup at the start always put a smile on Fred's face.

Fred Fine was the owner-operator of A Fine Motel in outback Queensland, Australia. He grew up as the son of a cattleman, raised on the land in a harsh climate. His father, Frank, had died in a farming accident in 1966, and afterwards, the incident was never spoken about by his family or friends.

Prior to Frank dying, Fred had enlisted in the army and was transported from Queensland south by bus, off to join other recruits at Kapooka, New South Wales, before his posting to what would be his new battalion and family: 2RAR, which was located in the North Queensland town of Townsville. He was there for the next ten years.

As a boy, then teenager, he knew his future on the farm was not likely, and the idea of adventure became something that sparked interest in leaving Harveston one way or another. He would say to his close mates – Johno, Bull and Arthur – that the army was 'an easy way out of this place', and whenever he trained either at high school or for sports, running along the road or up the moun-tains, he imagined he was chasing adventure over foreign lands. And to him, the army allowed him to do just that. It also helped that Johno was leaving town to join the army as well.

Fred and Johno had been best mates since the eighth grade, when they realised their mutual love for yabbying, practical jokes and rugby league. But mostly because Johno would knock the block off anyone at school if they teased Fred's sister, Beryl, for being different. The first and last time Beryl was called a 'spastic', Johno was close by and belted Alan Dixon so hard his front teeth were sent flying. Rumour had it they landed in Martha Bigsby's vanilla milkshake, and she almost choked on the last sip she sucked through her straw, not realising they fell in her cup.

The military came naturally to Fred, and once his skills became noticed, he was made lead scout of his section within the infantry platoon. His life on the land had laid the foundations for this role. With heightened awareness in skills such as dead reckoning, navigation, tracking, and vision through the scrub – being able to spot non-conforming objects like the outline of a body or the curve of a helmet – he was posted to Townsville in January 1967 and served for ten years. He began his first tour of Vietnam not long after arriving to 2RAR in May 1967, and he did another tour in June 1970.

While Fred was deployed to the war in Vietnam in 1967, he received a letter from his mother. He knew his mother's handwriting well; it was always so elegant. So, as he sat dug in at a small hill, Nui Dat, under a mackerel sky, the beauty of the shimmering cloud patterns above his head was lost on him, and his power of compartmentalisation was nowhere to be found as he read that Pearl had been forced to sell the cattle and most of the farm to pay off the debts they had incurred following Frank's death.

That day, he cried more than he ever did after losing mates to the Viet Cong – it had all become too much to bear. Pearl wrote: *It's with sadness that I need to tell you this, son. But I've subdivided and kept a plot of land beside the highway on the edge of town, and I'm using some of the money left over to build a motel for Beryl and me to run.'* Explaining further, she expressed that*: this will sustain an income for us after Frank's death.* She added: *I've decided to call the establishment A Fine Motel.*

It took months for Fred to draw a smile with that news. And why would he smile in the middle of war? The land he grew up on was just as much a part of him as the heart that was in his chest. He knew he didn't belong on the land in the way it was run, but he always wanted something more from it – there was 'unfinished business' there, he thought. But with the farm now in somebody else's possession, it was something he couldn't bring himself to return home for.

However, eventually, Fred began to miss home, and

things started getting harder for him to stay in the military, especially when his mother's care packages with her handwritten poems, melted Caramello Koalas and new cartoon books arrived. He became attached to the cartoon comic book: *Footrot Flats,* written by New Zealand Cartoonist Murray Ball, and they reminded him of home.

Having got his fill of adventure, his mind began to wander, and like an incarcerated man, he regularly dreamt of plans or ways to 'get out' of the army and build a new life with better monetary reward than he was used to. But ultimately, he had no idea how to make the exit.

The second tour of duty took its toll on Fred. He developed some things he'd refer to as 'tics': a constant ringing in both ears and a feeling of anxiety, accompanied with a nervous sneeze that would occur spontaneously. His dreams became vivid, and he'd wake in a pool of sweat, sometimes not knowing where he was. Feelings of undirected anger surfaced, but he managed to withhold that from most. 'Sergeant Fine's in a foul mood today, so stay out of his way' would be all that was said from his troops and fellow soldiers.

He would write letters home to his mum and sister, and after a while, he realised the satisfaction being creative gave him. In what he and other diggers referred to as 'downtime', he would put pen to paper, developing his wordsmithing ideas, documenting his thoughts to help take his mind away from the ugliness of war that surrounded him.

Upon his discharge – an 'inadvertent snuff out', he referred to it as – he ended up back home to somehow try to reclaim his place on the land and help his sister with the new family business, as his mum had passed, and by this time, he had accumulated dozens of poems and short stories.

Once he was back home, the following counter-productive years were spent reflecting on his past, consuming more and more alcohol, and walking aimlessly the one-mile trek to and from the pub, and wallowing in the wake of war and the unfortunate loss of his mother.

His sister, Beryl scared Fred one morning when she wheeled out onto the veranda to feed the kookaburras and found him passed out at the bottom of the stairs at the entry to the stumpy lowset house. So, she quietly reversed her wheelchair back inside the house and moved towards the kitchen.

Beryl grabbed the lemon-scented dish washing deter-gent bottle from the stainless-steel sink and wheeled back to the veranda. She looked at the label 'Morning Fresh, I give you morning fresh'she thought and aimed the bottle at Fred's head, squeezed it hard, a coagulated yellow blob landed on his ear. Next, she managed to grab the garden hose and unravel it from the steel tyre rim, put a kink in the hose, and then she turned the tap on full and finally succeeded in waking him – on that cold winter morning – with a blast of water, full pressure directly up his nose and at his face.

He woke, startled, coughing and splattering with bubbles gathering around the side of his hair and chest. And before he could come to his senses, the first thing he heard were the cackles of kookaburras, as if mocking him. It was his favourite bird; however, in that moment, he just felt their judgment.

The next thing he heard was Beryl.

She screamed at him, 'If you ever want to live in the present, you must stop reliving the past. So, get up and clean yourself.' She then finished with a cheap shot. 'You smell like a piss trough at a race meet.'

Fred looked around and realised he was laying on the ground next to the front veranda, unable to make it up the three stairs or utilise the wheelchair ramp a few hours earlier. He stared at the cheeky kingfishers, blowing the soap suds in the air as he responded with a slur, 'For god's sake, Beryl … I left town just after Dad died, and now I'm home and Mum's gone, and on top of that, I got kicked out of the army'.

'It was your decision to leave, Fred,' Beryl reminded him.

'Yeah. And now I'm back home.'

'That's right. Now you're back. And just what are you gunna do about it?'

Fred had all but forgotten how strong of a stink-eye Beryl was able to give when she was annoyed.

Beryl's words pierced Fred like hailstones shredding all leaves from a fruit tree in a storm, and this moment was enough to give Fred the wake-up call he needed. Though the feeling of being a failure still rested just below the surface, he used this fear to drive himself towards pragmatic change, recounting the many times his dad said to him, 'Your blood group is B positive for a reason, son'.

The wind turned and blew smoke into Fred's eyes, forcing him to turn away from a concentrated gaze into the flame that was now taking shape. As they had organised that morning, Fred was now at Johno's, out the backyard watching as Johno prepared the fire, and their evening meal.

'She's burning well,' said Johno, leaning forward to poke a small piece of ironbark into a better position. He stood up and shovelled some hot coals from the centre of the fire and poured them onto the lid of the iron camp oven. 'That lamb leg and potatoes will be about another hour.'

'You're such a firebug.' Fred flicked a pebble he picked from the ground after he sat down on the opposite side of the fire to Johno.

Johno raised his eyebrows. 'That's a bit rich ... I

blame you, Fred. Remember that ant nest in front of your old house? We must have been twelve years old, and it was your idea to funnel petrol down the ant hole.'

'I reckon we were thirteen,' Fred corrected, followed with, 'what else did you put in that camp oven?'

'That's right.' Johno pointed his fire poking stick at Fred. 'First year of high school, and that afternoon, you got sick of hearing your mum complain about the ants ruining her lawn. Just some carrots, onion, and a splash of Tecca's red wine.'

'Yeah, she hated those bloody ants. They were tough, and no matter what we did, they always came back.' Fred paused for a moment, and then his tone became serious. 'They'd probably been there longer than anyone else around these parts.'

'That was the first time I experienced the danger of fire, Fred, but also the power and beauty in it,' replied Johno.

Fred flicked another pebble at Johno. 'See! You *are* a bloody firebug!'

Johno stared into the flame and asked Fred, 'You name something else, then, that has the ability to take whatever stands in its way and—'

'How about water,' Fred interrupted.

Johno contemplated Fred's answer. 'Sure. Yes, water can too. I know that … but it just doesn't appeal to me as much, I guess.

'And that's what makes you a firebug, mate.'

'Well, hear me out now. Nobody has ever called water "alive" or "dead", in the way you'd describe fire.'

They both stared into the heart of the fire, admiring the brightness of the coals in the centre and the amber outline of a bluish flame that appeared twisting around a log.

'I'm not a "mad" firebug, mate … I'm "measured", maybe. An "enthusiast"? But not "mad". That poor kid that died in the Blunt Street house fire that night … What was his name?"

Fred crinkled his nose. 'Ahh … I'm not sure, Johno.'

'Darcy. I think, he was young Biddy's older brother …'

'Yeah, I heard about it from Townsville, and I heard more about the Whiskey Au Go Go blaze in Fortitude Valley that same week. The Bastard Bikies, fifteen people killed in that fire. It's hard to imagine'.

Johno agreed. 'Yeah, it was March 73, same week as … ah …' He was hesitant to speak true feelings, as it only brought back painful memories, but he persisted. 'I was in the Royal Brisbane Hospital after I broke my back down at Canungra with the army.'

'Bloody Nungas,' Fred chirped in.

Johno continued, 'Ha! Yeah … Nungas. Anyway, I could smell the smoke and almost taste the ash blowing through the hospital window the next morning when I woke up.'

'Shit aye, poor bastards.' Fred felt sorrow for the victims, and he and Johno were quiet for a minute. 'Let's get the camp oven out, so the meat can rest … it smells ready enough to me.'

When dinner was done and dusted, Fred realised he'd been staring into the flames for some time, contemplating his 'next moves'. He looked up into the black sky and took in the enormousness of The Southern Cross. Suddenly, he realised that enough was enough.

He turned to Johno and said, 'Hey, Johno, I reckon I'm going to get my shit together.'

Johno took a swig of his beer and replied, 'Oh yeah? That's good, mate.'

'I'm going to get a dog, ya know. There're some things I want to try doing for this town, and the motel, and I can't do it unless I'm clear-headed. I might even go get my head checked, by a quack and all?'

Johno stood up to put another piece of hardwood on the fire. 'Can't hurt, can it. Find out if you have half a brain.' He gave a wide grin before continuing, 'Hey, Jed Moreton's dog had a litter just recently, so maybe we could go check them out.'

Fred nodded eagerly. *Yep, now is the time*, he thought as he looked back up at the myriad stars and considered the potential that lay before him.

Chapter Three

THE ROUTINE

February 1981

Not only did Fred frequent Arthur's Bakery every Monday morning with Johno, for a meat pie at breakfast time, he always bought a dozen fresh free-range eggs from Arthur's wife, Margaret. Margaret's chooks wandered the streets surrounding the bakery, and whenever Fred saw those chickens, he had flashbacks of his childhood when his father killed some of their own chooks for dinner.

Fred had to hold the bouncing hessian bag of decapitated chickens while Frank chopped their heads off with an axe on an iron-bark wooden chopping stump. He remembered the bag being heavy for his six-year-old arms, and once, he dropped the bag and let the headless chickens loose. They jumped around the backyard, with Dad and the dog trying to catch them, while Mum was in the kitchen looking through the window and laughing loudly. Beryl still had use of her legs at that age and was chased by one of them, Frank told her 'Beryl, the chickens don't know what they are doing, it's just a shock-type reaction their body feel and they weren't chasing you at all'. It didn't help too much, she had nightmares for years and refused to eat chicken for a long time. Margaret's chickens were always put away at night, safe from the prowling foxes. Fred loved boiled egg sandwiches, and free-range eggs were the only way to go, in his opinion.

Before leaving home each Monday morning, Fred would remove a two dollar note from the motel's till and set off out the door. He enjoyed his weekly Monday morning stroll to the bakery with Johno. Breathing in the fresh air, he would usually think *this is going to be the week*. The week when someone big and famous would call to make a booking to stay at the motel and put him and his town on the map, which would ultimately help get it out of the decline it had been stuck in for some time.

He and Johno travelled along Sale Street next to the cattle yard markets, then down the laneway that took them to the back entrance roller door of the bakery. While on route, they discussed the weekend happenings.

Johno let Fred in on a secret he had been holding onto for a few weeks about how he was sleeping with the publican's wife, Jeanie. Johno told Fred about his rendezvous down the hill behind the sporting oval by the creek at night with Jeanie when publican Reg was working late. Fred chuckled nervously, then sneezed three times in close succession. He was worried for Johno because he knew Reg wouldn't think twice about busting Johno right in the kisser.

Johno looked at Fred after the sneezes and remarked, 'Mate, you gotta get that looked at … you're going to pop a vein in your forehead if that gets any worse.'

Fred told Johno that he had an appointment in the city with a psychologist. 'Yeah, I might even talk about the dreams I've been having with the faceless man sitting under a Moreton Bay fig tree.'

The dream had evolved over the years, but the constant thing he recalled was himself walking through a field and approaching a large tree. As he walked closer to the tree, he always saw a man who was wearing a wide-brim hat that sagged, but no matter how close he got to the man, or how he tried to look upon the man's face, the man moved as if he was on a lazy Susan.

Johno looked at Fred and agreed, 'Yep, that's a weird dream.'

As they continued to mosey along, Johno pointed out some new company vehicles that had been driving through Harveston, and they started talking about the rumours they'd heard about these new arrivals.

'I've heard people say they're looking for land to mine,' said Johno.

Fred screwed up his face. 'There's no gold left out here, though, so they must be looking for something else.'

'Some people say they're looking for coal,' Johno replied.

'Over my dead body is anyone putting a coal mine on this land,' exclaimed Fred, hands on his hips.

'Who knows, mate,' replied Johno, 'but it's a bit strange that they're all here, don't you think?'

Fred shrugged as they arrived at the bakery, and the topic of conversation was put on hold. It was now time for Fred to make his selection, which varied with his mood. It would be mushy peas, and beef when it was rainy or he was feeling down; curried pie when he lacked energy on a cold morning; and steak, cheese, and bacon if he was feeling lucky … and so on. He rubbed his hands together the way a salesman would when he knew he just hooked a customer.

Arthur always asked him the same question, 'Would you like my special squeeze sauce?' Arthur never liked the small-town lifestyle, but he loved the people and his family, which kept him there. He had been inventing quirky items and recipes, introducing them in the bakery for years. His latest one was a tiny plastic bottle filled with tomato sauce, which he sold for ten cents, to go with his savory baked goods.

But when he asked Fred if he would like sauce for an extra ten cents, Fred's consistent response, accompanied with a cheeky smile, was, 'No thanks, Arthur, I'm watching my sugar intake.'

To which Arthur replied, 'Come on, Fred, you're as thin as a post, and this is one of my best creations yet, mate.'

Fred, however, would shake his head as he adamantly turned the sauce down.

He had developed an aversion to spending money frivolously and discretely declined to pay the extra ten cents for the packet of squeeze sauce. And while he stared at the hand-written ten-cent sign taped onto the large ceramic bowl holding the tiny squeeze sauce bottles and salivated, he then felt his wallet inside his pants pocket and thought *no*. He only carried a two dollar note, and the pies cost eighty cents, with the dozen eggs costing $1.10, which only left ten cents in change.

When he got home, he would put the ten cents into a money jar and, making sure nobody was looking, he would pull out a small card that had twenty squares: four rows times five rows. On the twentieth square, he had written the words *Free Pie Day!* Fred implemented a similar scheme for repeat business at the motel for people who stayed over – every tenth overnight stay was free. In his mind, this was resulting in repeat business from the same patrons.

Fred's rule in the motel contract's fine print stated: *This can only be redeemed for single-night stays; not to be used in conjunction with consecutive nights.*

Once Fred and Johno made their selection of pies, they took their 'dog's eyes' to sit in front of the store, watching the cars travel by. Fred complained about it being laundry day back at the motel. He told Johno about the Kiwi guest he called 'The Shearer', and how he regularly found sheep droppings in the bathroom and among the bed sheets.

Johno, as usual, was quick to make a joke. 'Well, Fred, you know what a Kiwi's wife says to keep her husband on a cold night?'

'No, what?' asked Fred.

Johno replied, 'Come closer, baaa'be.'

Fred laughed and replied, 'Good one, but Johno, in all seriousness, you just never know what you're going to find between the sheets, you know? It's terrifying!' Fred sneezed.

Johno then chose to revisit the earlier conversation with Fred. 'Mate, you know what, I think there's something going on with all these new vehicles coming into town lately.'

Fred looked at Johno for a few seconds, waiting to clear his mouth before replying, 'Yeah, I reckon there is too. You know I have a guy that stays at the motel once a month who claims to be a gold prospector, but it's weird that Sintex are the company on the cheques he pays with. I thought they only did cattle and timber … I might be able to hit him with a few questions to see what he has to say.'

Johno chimed in, saying, 'I think I've seen him opening gates going into Uncle Jack's place. Ain't no gold out there, that's for sure. What's that guy's name?'

Fred contemplated it for a second. 'Devon Cruickshank, I reckon.'

Johno looked thoughtful. 'Okay, see what this Cruickshank fella reckons next time he's at the motel. Sounds suss to me, mate.'

Fred nodded with agreeance.

Chapter Four

THE BIG IDEA #1

April 1981

Harveston was just east of red earth and was the heart of the peanut farming region, surrounded by waterways leading into dams and catchments, with some dry sandy creeks that would only ever run during the rainy season.

Even though Fred had been in a 'pot-shot' state of mind, and at times a drunken stupor for the past few years, he remained observant with the goings-on around Harveston. He loved his town and wanted nothing more than positive change while attempting to help get it on the map, bringing wanted attention and attracting tourists with fat wallets to boost the local economy.

He had been aware of the slow decline of productivity, coupled with the exodus of some families after property sales to a silent buyer. And the only information the town's people had been able to gather was that the company buying all the properties was Sintex, which was said to be one of Australia's largest up-and-coming beef cattle producers, secondary to a logging company.

Many rumours circulated around the town as to what Sintex's intentions may be, for some had 'heard' that they also mined.

Fred even noted new faces driving big 'company-style' vehicles that regularly booked multiple rooms at the motel, and he was slightly suspicious about their activity. However, he was yet to formally inquire as to what they were doing or where their interests lay in his peaceful tiny town.

Fred ruminated on many things, but mostly on what might help bring the people in, and the best idea to enter his mind, so far, was placing a statue of a big peanut, still in its shell, on top of the motel and adding a tagline below in red block letters: A Fine Motel – Home of the Big Nut!

In Fred's mind, this would be something tourists would drive from far and wide to see, and instead of driving through the town non-stop, leaving only dust behind, they would park and spend money at one of the shops or stay overnight at his motel. Then they could do daytrip adventures in the surrounding beautiful spots.

When Fred described this idea to the other locals, he would refer to it as 'a baited hook'. He would say, 'We have all the bait surrounding this place, but what we're missing is a hook to catch people's attention to land them on the line.'

At the bar one night, when one of his mates, Bull, quizzed him on how the town was supposed to do that, Fred replied, 'We have enough natural resources out here to attract tourists, we just need to get some attention to draw them in.'

Bull queried, 'How do you suppose we do that, Fred'?

'I dunno yet, mate, but I'm working on it … You know that Brisbane is hosting the Commonwealth Games next year, so we'll have a tourism boom.'

Bull scratched the stubbly hair on his jawline, then said, 'Games? What bloody games?'

The Commonwealth Games, mate,' Fred replied. 'The Queen will probably be here for it, ya know.'

Bull replied, 'Well, Fred, let's say we land these so-called "fish on the hook", then whado we do with 'm?'

Fred looked up at the ceiling fan slowly spinning, noticing a thick layer of dust on the rusty blades, and he took a moment before answering, 'Well, I guess we reel them in, mate.'

Bull asked, 'And how do ya suppose we do that, aye?'

Fred shrugged. 'Ehhh, I haven't got that far yet, but I reckon we get some media-type attention, like get on the news on *A Current Affair,* or something. Get Ray Martin out here, I reckon … the ladies love him.'

Bull started to chuckle and replied, 'Righto, Fred.'

Then he called to the publican, 'Hey, Reg! Fred's had enough for today.'

Over the following weeks, there was some to-ing and fro-ing with the town's folk and some of the regular guests of the motel, especially with Tom – The Shooter – Neilson. Fred respected The Shooter's ideals and life decisions. Tom believed the 'Big Nut' was a good idea, and to receive praise or acceptance from Tom held a lot of weight. Although Fred liked Tom's advice and conversation, he sure as hell never looked forward to the mess he had to clean up in the motel room after Tom had left town.

Arthur also agreed that the idea had merit; however, he was pushing for Fred to call the motel The Big Bun, after his 'famous fruit bun'.

Reg suggested The Big Beer, but Reg didn't even brew his own beer, so Fred reckoned it wouldn't tie in with the town's surroundings or the people in it.

Fred remembered back to the breakfast table as a boy, and the smell of coffee and burnt toast entered his mind. That's where the family would all be together for at least one meal for the day. He listened to his father say to his mother when she would complain about someone else's beliefs conflicting with hers, 'Opinions are like arseholes; everyone's got one.'

And Fred agreed that it was a fair point.

Fred could see how the Big Nut would give something extra to Harveston, something to entice tourists into the local land and exploring the other wonders the area had to offer, like panning for gold when the creeks were running, and fossicking in the old goldfields, freshwater lakes, and taking a wine tour of Frenchy's vineyard – so he decided to go for it.

Excitedly, he searched the yellow pages for an artist to come up with a design for the statue of the Big Nut. The phone call with them was short and sharp after he realised it would cost $300 for what he needed, plus it would mean a trip to Brisbane for a meeting, which he'd rather not attend. Three hundred dollars wouldn't break the bank; however, he wasn't about to give one month's profit away to the first person he spoke to. So, in trying to save a dollar, he decided to enquire with the publican's wife, Jeanie.

Jeanie did all the designs for the skirting boards that ran around the veranda of the pub. The skirtings were mostly made up of the favourite yellow-labelled local beer with four Xs prominently displayed just above head height.

It had just past Anzac Day, and Fred headed to the pub to speak to Jeanie. Johno was already there when Fred arrived.

Fred bought a round of drinks, and he and Johno sat on a bar stool in the corner, not far from the jukebox. Johno walked over and placed a coin in the slot and looked at the songs on the list. He mainly loved Australian rock music and made a beeline to find his favourite Cold Chisel song 'Standing on the Outside'.

The opening chords of the guitar being strummed by Ian Moss rattled in a quick, upbeat way, and Johno got the same feeling inside as he did on any Friday afternoon when work was finished for the week. Johno let out a *'woo!'* before he pirouetted around and sashayed back over to the table, feeling like he'd made a hero's choice song selection. Within thirty-seconds of Johno sitting back at the table, he and Jeanie started playing footsies with each other while Fred pitched the Big Nut idea.

Johno was lip-syncing to the opening phases of the song and decided to sing at full blast when it came to (in his mind) the first rhythmically then with confidence when he knew the lyrics: *'Doo-do-doo de-be-do-be-de-doo buy a twenty-two, shoot the whole thing down!'*

Fred and Jeanie both stopped talking and stared at Johno.

Fred asked him, 'You right, mate?'

Johno nodded, with his face crumpled as he mimicked Jimmy Barnes' singing animation.

Fred and Jeanie then picked up and continued their discussion again.

Jeanie agreed to create the statue for Fred and said she could do it for half the price he was quoted over the phone. 'You see, Fred, my dear, it's all about texture and visualisation of what you really want, and I can feel the concept coming through you like beer from the tap into the schooner of my mind ...'

Jeanie continued talking, but Fred's mind started to wander off with unhelpful introspection of failure and hopelessness. The ringing in his ears became the only thing he could hear. He sneezed into his beer, blowing froth over the table, and some landed on Jeanie's shoulder.

Johno also copped some, and he wiped his cheek and slightly raised his left eyebrow.

Everyone in the bar ignored the mess, all knowing Fred suffered from 'shellshock', and they carried on with whatever they were doing, mostly watching the footy, or playing pool.

Fred, by no means, agreed to commissioning the piece, but his actions were not in line with what was going on inside his mind. He inadvertently gave Jeanie the wrong impression by smiling and nodding in her general direction that he was happy to move forward with the Big Nut statue, and she believed he had given her the green light, with free rein on any decisions needed along the way.

Chapter Five

THE TOWN

May 1981

Harveston was nestled in between heavily wooded valleys with towering mountainous ridge lines. Bees buzzed to loud hums, and the ringing of cicadas formed a harmony among the golden wattles and gums that followed the veiny roads that wound around the region. The bird life whistled, whipped, cackled and called at the crack of dawn when the sun peaked over the Rocky Mountains far off in the east.

Fred could never work out why the laughing kookaburra, for the most part, found humour as the sun went to bed. The big-beaked kingfisher birds nested their eggs in brown dirt termite mounds a few metres off the ground to keep their chicks safe from stealthy land predators, such as the dusty red fox or the forever-scavenging goanna. In the creeks and dams surrounding the town, fish were easily caught when a line was dropped from the bank or off a bridge. Silver and golden perch, saratoga, and barramundi could be found if you knew where to look over by green river, and Fred thought himself fortunate when he reeled in a catch off the water's edge.

It also was rich in all-but-forgotten ancient history, which was mostly dark from the last one hundred years or so. And there were only whispers of what now felt like past mysteries circulating from time to time, usually to inform newcomers of 'you know what really went on here'. The credence was clear, done with somewhat shameful undertones on what occurred in the past years when European settlers first established the area, and it continued in some cases until only decades earlier.

The Aboriginal elders would recount stories to Bull when he was young, stories of the mass poisonings of the local tribes, and rituals surrounding the bora ring and kippa ring that existed on the north. 'Follow the Emu Creek line for a few hours, and when you get to an open patch of land nearby, four tall bunya nut trees standing above the rickety bridge over Sandy creek is where the *bora ring* sits.' Bull passed this secret onto Fred and Johno when they were teenagers, and the three of them travelled on foot to explore. And he made Fred and Johno promise not to tell anyone, otherwise he would get in trouble if it ever got back to the elders.

When the boys followed the track to the sacred site,

they found the large volcanic rocks of the bora and kippa rings. The largest stone in the middle stood tall as any adult, if not taller, and the smaller dark-purple-grey rocks had been placed evenly in a circle around the centre.

Bull told Fred and Johno, 'Don't enter the circle … leave it for the elders. We can just look.'

The rings were twenty metres apart, and Bull pointed out the kippa ring. 'That one over there's for the teenagers, and that one over there's for the adults.'

It was a stunning place, and Fred looked at the rocks then around the hillside to admire the trees and positioning of the site. The running creek had a water hole, which the boys decided to have a swim in. The rock formations made a good platform for jumping from into the cool freshwater pool. Only when it flooded, like in January 1974, did it become epically dangerous to navigate, especially if one were to put themself in harm's way.

Just as The Great Dividing Range split the land and sea, the same was said of the affect that large amounts of rainfall had on the country lands when compared to the city; it was vastly different.

Harveston was built in and around slow-trickling creeks and streams that flowed into the main river, which ran north to south and eventually into holding dams for the state capital, Brisbane. The grass was brown most of the year, but a sprinkle of rain would turn it green with ease. When it rained for days, the waterways swelled to a size without concern, and the locals were happy with lush fields, full dams and creeks that would eventually turn to a run instead of a slow dribble. When the rain didn't stop after days, the creeks became thick waterways and flowed into each other to form larger catchments that threatened livestock, houses, shops, and even cut the locals off from the rest of civilisation. Food supplies would be okay for a time, for each household knew how to conserve or skint, due to their upbringing in a time when three meals a day was rare.

At one point in its history, Harveston was also rich in minerals, though it had not been seriously mined for anything in years. The last time was more than eighty years ago at the tail end of the gold rush. The unfinished railway line remained in place, crossing over gullies following the highway from the east into town, stopping short before the last creek crossing on the edge of town. Some prospectors still fossicked on large parcels of land, but these were more weekend hobbies, and nobody gave much thought to them.

In recent years, much like Fred, though for different reasons, Harveston had been on the brink of collapse. The rusted corrugated roofs of the houses, which also had crusted paint peeling from the weatherboard walls were prominent and easily seen through the dusty car windows of passers-by driving past the delipidated shops in the main street, rarely stopping for food or fuel.

During this time, Fred observed that the bush was the only steadfast thing able to weather the drought or flood. It had seen challenging times, but its beauty remained.

Some local farmers continued to sell off large lots of land to Sintex. It was the opinion that Sintex could bring jobs to the area when they established business in town. Nobody knew who owned Sintex, they just noticed the fleet of brand-new white Land Cruisers that came into town on a monthly basis and stayed at Fred's motel. They kept to themselves and were usually aloof whenever asked how things were progressing getting their cattle brought in, or if they would buy from the local stockyard sales.

Some families had moved away, which made some remaining townsfolk slightly sad, uncertain, and nervous for the town's future. This was mostly ignored though, with people deciding to carry on with day-to-day life, holding a stiff upper lip with true country spirit, but possibly more were pretending and had hope that everything was going to be okay. But the underlying sentiment was anxiety, and the worry was seen in some glassy eyes, even when replying to a simple question, 'How you going?' with the typical answer, 'Can't complain, nobody's gonna listen.'

Fred often felt slightly responsible when he left the town at a time the property he grew up on needed someone to take over its production to carry on the family business.

Fred's family and mates, to his knowledge, were not

religious by any means, but some property owners were seen to be when you approached Harveston from the east. The three signs on the left side of the road, spaced 500 metres apart, quoted religious text and connotation. One sign read: *Jesus replied, 'Very truly I tell you, no one can see the kingdom of God without being born again.* Another sign read: *If you love me, you will save my commandments.* And there was another: *Even to your old age, I am he, and even to grey hairs, I will carry you!*

Oh, how Fred hated those signs! Often, they would be target practice for passers-by with either guns or empty beer bottles.

On the right-hand side of the highway, for about three kilometres before the beginning of town, was where Frank Fine's property lay, and it hugged all along the way to the edge of the boundary next to the regular quarter-acre house blocks that ran parallel to the main street of town. The highway pierced straight through the middle of the town, clearly dividing the houses on the right side and shops on the left when driving east to west.

When Fred was a boy, the town only had a pub, a mechanic, a grocery store, and a petrol station. In the years that followed, the town grew slowly, and more variety came along. It now had its own bank; a Chinese restaurant called Ming's – Sue Lee and her family moved into Harveston in 1973; the bakery that Arthur King built in 1972; an ex-meat worker turned butcher, Jed Moreton, established Eat Moreton Meat, also in 1972; a rural store run by the Country Co-op; and in 1977, a 'swank shop' called The Boutique Antique, owned by a Frenchman by the name of Tequil Le' Fur, who planted a vineyard and also took up residence in a half-broken stone house not far when travelling west out of town. And since Sintex came to town, a 'massage parlour' had opened across from Fred's motel.

Despite all these businesses attempting to grow the town's local economy, they weren't like the feathers of a male peacock, failing to attract newcomers. The roads were dirt, and the sports oval tucked behind the shops had a small, white-painted weatherboard grandstand on one side with the change rooms on the opposite side. The grass in between was coloured light green with brown patches for the best part of the year until the rainy season came and gave some cushioning for those playing football on the oval.

The houses to the right through town did not run directly alongside of the road. Right of the road sat two tennis courts surrounded by rusted wire fencing, car parks and a small park with climbing equipment for children, which ended up being more like a graveyard for a tractor than an area to play in – no one was even sure whose idea it was to place it there.

However, the locals loved their town and supported it in any way they could, though more often than not, keeping their heads above water was the main priority.

But right now, the issues facing the town were bigger than anyone could recall from recent history, and nobody knew exactly what was needed to turn things around. Until of course, Fred Fine returned home and decided to clean up his act.

Chapter Six

LIKE CATS AND DOGS

December 2023

Johno woke early to beat the traffic. It had started raining the day before and not stopped all night. He was driving down to visit Fred in hospital and knew that people tended to go loopy driving in the rain.

Fred was asleep when he arrived, so he decided to get a coffee in the café downstairs. He stood in line listening to the people before him order their food. 'Pesto,' he said to himself. 'What's pesto?'

A young woman joined the queue behind him with her two children and waited patiently.

Johno heard the young boy say, 'Mum, did you get the *Footrot Flats* magazines for Grandad?'

'Yes, dear,' she replied.

Johno huffed then turned to get a closer look at them. He squinted and asked, 'Is that you, Julie Fine?'

'Oh, hello, Mr Johnson, fancy seeing you here.'

Johno looked down at Maggie and Atticus. 'Yep, I thought I should come say hi to your grandad for Christmas.'

Julie replied, 'Yes, we came last week and back again to see the old coot' then she paused. 'Would you like to sit with us while we wait?'

'Sure, that sounds good,' replied Johno, following the Fine family to a table and some chairs in the corner. 'It's coming down like cats and dogs out there, isn't it, boy,' he remarked to Atticus as he took a seat.

'Sure is,' replied Atticus. He then appeared pensive before asking, 'Hey, Mr Johnson, do you know who the Jerky Boys were?'

Johno looked up from taking a sip on his hot coffee. 'Gee, I haven't heard that in a while. And yes, I do know, in fact, and actually, all this rain reminds me of the Jerky Boy Mick. He used to help me with the water truck and once told me a story after he had finished school for the day about the floods of 1974.'

Atticus sat up straight, looking eager to hear what Johno had to say.

Johno looked at Julie.

She glanced down at the time on her phone and said, 'I think we've got time … maybe the old man is getting a good sleep with the rain on the roof.'

Johno nodded and said, 'Okay, so let me remember correctly … it was just into the start of the new year in 74 when …'

Chapter Seven

THE BIG FLOOD

January 1974

Timmo looked at his lunch, and then over at his friend Biddy's lunchbox. 'Friggin' hell, I'm sick of corned meat … I'll swap you my corned meat sandwich for your tuna sandwich?'

Biddy shook his head. 'Nah, not today, but you can have my apple for your banana, if you like?'

Timmo looked at the bruised banana then bit into his sandwich and said, 'Nah, I'm good.'

The boys chewed their stale white-bread sandwiches, and then Timmo said, 'Wonder what Mick is doing today?'

Biddy made a circle shape with his thumb and index finger then whacked it on his nose a couple of times.

'What's that mean?' asked Timmo.

'Fuck nose, but he's sure as hell not having to listen

to boring-arse Mr Ford yabba on in class at least. Did you see him spit when he was talking about Pythagoras? I won't ever sit in the front row of his class.'

Timmo laughed. 'Yeah, I saw it all right, almost hit Jenny in the head.' He finished his sandwich and wiped the white breadcrumbs from the corner of his mouth before suggesting, 'Let's go check out the creek before the bell rings.'

It had been raining for seven consecutive days, and the school bus wasn't able to make it into Harveston. Their primary school had under fifty kids, with combined classes to make up the numbers.

Mick loved the floods; he got to have the day off school and walk around the land and experience the power of water in nature. The creek that ran through Mick's parents' land was dry all year round, unless it rained like this. Three hills channelled water from their valleys down the gorge, creating waterfalls and rapids that pushed downstream any debris left from the last flood.

Mick stood by the water, watching it carve a new shape to the creek bank. He arrived home for lunch, wet and muddy. He walked onto the front veranda and could hear the radio playing in the kitchen. He wasn't surprised, as it was rarely off and always tuned into 4KQ radio. The song he heard playing was 'Have You Ever Seen Rain?'

by Creedence Clearwater Revival. He commented to his mum how fitting the song was, saying, 'I wonder if the band wrote it during a flood?'

In January 1974, the floods that hit the region were ones to break all rainfall events ever recorded to date, or to be recorded for many decades that followed.

Mick's mother, Joan, had hot creamy chicken soup ready to warm him up and made fresh bread to toast then break and crumble into the bowl. The powerful vision Mick had just seen of the water tearing apart the creek bank was like the toast in the soup, and he was silent while listening to John Fogerty's raspy voice sing the chorus of the song.

The phone rang, and Mick's dad, Colin, went to the office to answer it.

Mick, therefore, could only hear one side of the conversation.

'Hello?' his dad answered.

'Ah, not good …'

'Over the back, you say?'

'Yeah, that's getting too close to her, for sure.'

'Okay, leave it with me. I'll go see if she's okay. See ya, mate.' He hung up the phone and returned to the kitchen, taking his place back at the table.

'Who was that?' Joan asked.

Colin looked at them both. 'Rob Rouse, he reckons old Mrs Hooper could be stuck in her place, and the water is coming up fast around her. I'll have to go check on her.'

'I'll come with you, Dad.' Mick sat up straight, and his eyes lit up with the whiff of adventure.

Joan butted in quickly, 'If you're going, don't be doing anything stupid, you got it?'

Mick nodded. 'I won't, Mum.'

'And listen to ya father.' She quickly kissed him on the forehead.

'I'll go get the boat ready, you go get the truck and back it up,' said Colin.

They both placed their spoons on the table and drank the soup from their bowls. Mick's stomach was warm, for now, but he knew that wouldn't last long.

Mrs Hooper's house was on the flats below Mount Bunya, and it easily flooded with more than a few inches of rain.

'We've had fourteen inches over the last week, so the water's bound to be getting close to her floorboards,' Mick said to his dad.

'We'll have to take the sniggin' track along the topside of the mountain and then cut across the old Murphy place to make it close enough to drop the boat in,' Colin replied.

They took the slippery, poorly made road that was cut into the hill. The rain fell harder onto their raincoats, so hard the drops became like bullets hitting tin helmets, and Mick thought about the men from town who fought in the war in Vietnam.

It soon became obvious to Colin and Mick that if they did make it to Mrs Hooper's place, they probably wouldn't be able to make it back easily.

Eventually, they made it around the slope onto the road that led to the Murphy's place. The Murphy's lived in Brisbane and never used their property for anything, as far as Mick could tell, and he treated it like an extension of his block for adventures. This road took them to the dam where they lowered the boat into the water.

When the boat got closer into the water, Colin asked Mick to jump out of the car and prep for launch.

Mick first undid the wire fastened to the front of the trailer, then removed the tie-down straps and made sure the bung was in place and tight. As he did this, he accidentally knocked the bung out and it fell into the water. Mick dropped to the ground and put his head under the water to try and see the bung, not wanting to call out to his dad for help. So, he frantically felt around to find it.

'Are you ready back there?' Colin called.

Just then, Mick felt the bung and grabbed it tight and screwed it back into place so no water would enter the boat. 'Phew, yep, you can go now,' he called out to his dad.

Once the boat was in the water, Colin took the four-wheel drive and trailer, and then he made sure it was parked on higher ground, up nearby an old logger's loading ramp.

As they approached old Mrs Hooper's place in the tinny, they could see how high the water had come so far. The Moreton Bay fig branchers in the front yard now hung only a meter from the water, they laid back in the boat to avoid colliding with their heads. The water was well over the veranda floorboards and inside the house when they arrived. The water was deep enough that Mick's dad was able to take the boat up to the veranda and tie it off on the pole out front, just like they would at any regular jetty.

They called out to Mrs Hooper and heard a voice from around the back. Mick jumped out and waded through the water inside the house to find old Mrs Hooper sitting on her kitchen bench holding her cat and guineafowl with her blind, old German shepherd dog sitting next to her. 'Hey, Mrs H, we gotta go now. Dad's got the boat here, and the water's coming up fast.'

She replied, 'I'm not going anywhere without my animals.'

Mick looked around at the animals. 'Okay, I think we have room.' He took the cat, which scratched his fore-arms, and carried it above his head before placing it in the boat.

Colin held its scruffy wet neck while Mick returned for the dog and carried it, passing it to Colin in the boat.

On his last trip to the house, he took Mrs Hooper by the hand and led her out while she held onto her guineafowl under her arm.

Finally, when they were all safely in the boat and ready to go, Mrs Hooper cried out, 'Wait! I need my albums.'

Mick and his dad looked at each other.

'Okay, where are they?' Mick asked.

'On top of the cupboard in my room,' she said.

Mick jumped from the boat and swam into the house to grab the albums, and then he quickly returned to the boat.

All six of them just fit snug in the tinny.

As they rode out, they looked back at the house and could see the now massive body of water surrounding her quaint cottage. They ducked their heads again to avoid contact with the thick arm like branches of the Moreton Bay fig, which looked to be propped up at points by the water.

'Frigg'n hell! Watch that power line, Dad,' Mick said, and they lowered their heads to avoid a possible zap. 'What's with the guineafowl, Mrs H?' he asked.

She responded softly, 'She's the only one left from a dozen I had to start … goannas or wild dogs got the rest.'

Mick thought it strange to want to take that bird when so many other valuables could have been saved.

~

Biddy and Timmo sat in class. The rain was so heavy on the iron roof, they were unable to hear Mr Ford speak. They both looked out the window in wonder of what mischief Mick might be getting up to while they were forced to listen to Mr Ford 'blabber on' about Roman numerals or some theory about pie.

'I'd love a steamy hot meat pie right about now,' Biddy said to Timmo.

'Ford would probably spit all over it … He's on fire today.'

Mr Ford quickly interrupted, 'Quiet, you two … Now, the nine times table. Does anyone know a way to cheat by using your hands?'

Biddy looked around to find nobody had their hand up.

Mr Ford continued, 'If you can't do it fast enough in your head, you can use your hands. Five times nine equals … what?'

The kids looked at each other, but not a hand in the class went up fast enough before the teacher carried on, smugly, 'Look at your hands, palms towards your face, and curl the fifth finger … and there's your answer.' He turned away from the class to hold his hands up, showing four fingers on his left hand and five on his right. 'Forty-five, can you see? Try it again on another equation.'

Timmo looked down at his missing fingers; his right peripheral could see Biddy's cheeks bulged and eyebrows raised. Timmo had nothing else to say but, 'Frig off, Biddy.'

Chapter Eight

MILK MOUSTACHE

December 2023

Atticus sipped on his hot milo. 'Those boys sound pretty wild … aye, Mum.'

'Oh yes, they were.' She looked fondly at Johno. Can I tell Mr Johnson my poem before I give it to Grandad?' Atticus asked his mother. 'Okay, I think Dad will be awake now, so we'll go up after. Wipe your mouth, Atti.'

Atticus took out a folded piece of paper, opened it up and began to read.

'It's just called woof for now.' He announced.

Woof

Outside I heard our red dog barking.
Jessie! What is the matter?

Behind Maggie's pink scooter against the rock,
Hid a blue tongue lizard, puffed up and frightened.

Its scaly skin of greens, blacks, and browns,
I went for the rake and gently picked it up.

Tongue hissed tail curled its legs gripped on tight,
As I carried it up by the cubby house fence.

And plopped it over landing on the soft grass,
Allowing it to continue its very own path.

'I like it' said Johno, 'reminds me of a dog your Grandad had called Jessie when we were younger, get him to tell you about her one day.'

'Sure thing. You come up with us, Mr Johnson,' said Atticus as he reached out to take Johno's hand.

Johno smiled widely and replied, 'Absolutely, my boy.' And he took Atticus' small, smooth hand in his larger, once-calloused hand.

Chapter Nine

THE BIG IDEA #2

May 1981

Once a year, Harveston had a sausage festival in town, which Fred's mother Pearl used to enter her homemade venison and wallaby sausages, usually with a win every year. Locals came from far and wide to sell and compete for the trophy of best local snag, and travellers flocked to the town to taste some of the best meats around the state.

So, in line with Fred's first big idea, he reckoned that maybe it would be worth adding a statue of a big snag and a catchphrase to the motel, such as, 'Home of the Big Snag'.

After talks, mainly with Johno this time, Johno suggested visiting Mal on Friday afternoon – Mal was the local taxidermist who lived in the hills just outside of town – to see if he could make a mould for a large sausage to be placed on top of the motel.

They jumped into Fred's gold-speckled Holden HZ Kingswood station wagon and drove out to see him.

'Haven't been this far out in the sticks for a while,' Fred said.

Johno looked across at Fred, replying, 'Yeah, mate, Mal is an old bushman … apparently, he moved up from the Blue Mountains after his wife left him, and now he just wants to live off-grid.'

'Fair enough,' replied Fred, and he changed the subject. 'What do you know about palm trees, Johno?'

'Not much, mate, but I had the ABC on the other night, and *Landscape* was on the box. They reckon the coco palm is a fast-growing hardy plant that adapts well to our climate.'

Fred pondered out the car window for a minute. 'Right, I might stop in at the nursery on the highway next time I head to the city. They might look good around the front of the motel, you think?'

They arrived at the front gate placed at the bottom of a heavily wooded hill. Johno jumped out to open the gate, and Fred drove through. When Johno closed the gate behind him, it dragged through the dirt and locked with a horseshoe through a steel ring. The sign on the gate said: *NO ENTRY. Trespassers will be shot!*

It was a long, undulating rocky road with washouts forming a gutter from heavy rain on the high side of the track. It sent them deep into the woods where the canopy was so thick it was hard to make out the time of day.

As they pulled up next to the old shanty shed Mal worked in, the first thing Fred spotted was buckets piled on top of one another with overflowing thick coarse salt. Fred could only imagine this must have been what snow looked like. Next, Fred noticed the smell of drying blood and bone with what looked like off-cut animal hides laying in a heap against the base of the corrugated tin wall of the shed.

They entered, and Johno introduced Fred to Mal.

Mal had moved to town around ten years earlier while Fred and Johno were on deployment to Vietnam. He soon became busy with the demand for taxidermy for all the local hunters and those that came out from the city to hunt on a friend's property, either for sport or the opportunity to kill a deer for the unique-flavoured meat: venison.

After pleasantries, Fred asked, 'Hey, Mal, have you seen that new white Land Cruiser getting around town? His name's Cruickshank, and I think he's up to somethin'.'

Mal shook his head. 'Not really, Fred. I don't get out much, in case you can't tell.'

Fred replied, 'Well, if you see him, just keep a close eye on what he's up to.'

Johno then proceeded to explain Fred's idea of the Big Snag to Mal.

There was an intense discussion about the size, style and colour the Big Snag would be.

Fred stipulated, 'It can't look like a penis, whatsoever!'

Johno commented with a cheeky grin on his face, 'It could be tricky to pull that off,'

But Mal was confident that it could be done.

Fred then paused for a moment before he said, 'Yeah, ahh, what sort of price would something like that be?'

Mal was looking directly at Fred; however, Fred was distracted with the expression on one of the stuffed animal heads mounted on the wall behind Mal. The eyes appeared to be looking at him, making Fred feel weird about the whole situation. His ears began to ring louder than usual, and he noticed that dozens of animal heads on the wall were all looking at him. His eyes searched around for the exit and found that above the door was a large double-eight pointer stag with its mouth open, making the statement, *You're never going to amount to anything in life, Fred. Your fate will be met when you're all alone in woods behind the motel, just like mine did. Beware of the yowie!*

Fred sneezed and felt the need to get out of the room as soon as possible, replying to Mal, 'Sure, mate, it sounds good,' neglecting to say that he would have a think on the price of the statue, and then he rushed outside to get back in the car.

Johno followed and jumped in the car, thanking Mal as he closed the car door.

They travelled back to town, and Johno could tell Fred was noticeably quiet after the meeting. Fred eventually told Johno he was slightly disturbed and freaked out by the talking deer head on the wall.

Johno wasn't sure what to say, so he chose – 'with a silent country trait' – to leave him be and not question anything.

Fred finally decided to broach another topic. 'Bull also thinks something's going on with that man Cruickshank being in town. I'm not sold on him either, but when I asked him what he was in town for, he just said he was a prospector coming out to fossick in his spare time. But as I told you, Sintex pay his motel bills, so I think we need to find out more about what that company is doing here, because I don't think they're just buying land, cattle and timber.'

Chapter Ten

RICHARD 'JOHNO' JOHNSON

June 1981

Johno and Fred joined the army together just after Fred's father died. Johno enlisted as a combat engineer. His most common response to the warrant officer when in trouble was, 'But, sir, it's not my fault I got caught.'

And if you asked Johno what he learnt in the army, it would be how to build roads and blow stuff up.

While he was doing engineer training school post-recruit at Kapooka, his unit was doing a live-fire obstacle course after completing a weeklong field training exercise out bush. They were all extremely sleep-deprived, and during one part of the obstacle course, they were required to throw a hand grenade down range.

So, they all ran up, one by one to the mound of dirt, and needed to follow their corporal's orders of dropping the grenade pin and throwing the grenade down range.

When it was Johno's turn, he ran up to the mound and pulled the pin, but he was so nervous that he dropped the grenade and threw the pin.

The corporal quickly grabbed the grenade to throw it over the edge of the barrier, yelling, 'GO GO GO', and pushing Johno into the safety bay.

After the explosion, the corporal called, 'STOP! STOP! STOP!'

Everyone was ordered to file into position, and they ran into line.

Corporal Vic Dunkley looked Johno up and down and screamed at him, 'What's your name, private?'

'Private Johnson, corporal,' Johno replied.

'No! Your first name?' Corporal Dunkley screamed.

'Richard, corporal,' said Johno.

Corporal Dunkley said, 'You're telling me your parents inadvertently named you Dick Dick?'

Johno hesitated, pondering what had never been brought to his attention about his name before: 'Richard' and 'Johnson' were both terms used for … 'Yes, I guess so, corporal.'

Corporal Dunkley replied, 'Well, private, why do you think they named you in that way? Is it because you are a dick to the power of two?'

Johno paused before replying, 'Well, corporal, maybe it's because it's better to have two dicks than one.'

Corporal Dunkley looked Johno dead in the eye, their

noses almost touching. He yelled in his face, with saliva hitting Johno in the eye, 'Well, I think your new name is going to be Two Dicks … so, how do you feel about that?'

'Good, corporal! I like Two Dicks, corporal!' yelled Johno.

'I'm sure you do, private. Now, training is OVER! Everyone is on brass patrol. And if I find one loose shell, you'll all be running back to base, stretcher-carrying Private Two Dicks. You got that, 1 Section?'

They all cried out in unison, 'Yes, corporal!'

Johno attempted living in the city after his medical discharge from the army, but in the end, he moved back to the bush to avoid the struggle and strife of urban life. Now he was back home after his time in the military with one tour of duty to Vietnam. He worked as a water truck driver and wastewater operator — or 'shit-truck' operator, as he liked to call it. He was also a bit of a snoop; the kind of guy who was most likely to open your medicine cabinet at a party. In the same way, he liked to see what was in people's septic tanks, then tell stories at the pub about it!

All for a good laugh, of course.

Every Tuesday, sixteen-year-old Mick worked with Johno as part of paid work experience. Johno was well aware that Mick and his mates usually got up to mischief but always seemed to claw their way out of deep trouble and land on their feet.

Mick was Johno's gateway to a younger self, and they bonded over cricket and music. Mick and the rest of the Jerky Boys regularly trekked to Brisbane, either to party or play sport, and Mick always brought back a new cassette tape to share with Johno.

Johno waited outside the school in the shit-truck at 1 pm for Mick to arrive. He was listening to the cricket on the truck radio. The third test match of the Ashes international test was being played at Leed's cricket ground in London.

The English commentator was talking about the pigeons and not so much about the cricket when Mick walked down the dirt school path and hopped in the truck, saying, 'Hi.'

Johno replied, 'Shhh, I wanna hear what this pigeon does. England have us on the rails in this one.'

They sat there for another five minutes, waiting for the cricket to start again, both listening to the commentators focus on the pigeon's antics.

As they drove off, Johno said to Mick, 'Has the Jerky Boy eaten lunch yet?'

Mick replied, 'Not yet,' and then he pulled his latest cassette tape from the side pocket of his school bag, proudly waving it in front of Johno's face. 'It's Men at Work, just like us,' he said, passing it to Johno.

Johno took his eyes off the road to glance at the cassette and read *Business as Usual*. 'You're not wrong there, mate. Let's have a listen after we get you some food, aye?'

They stopped at the servo, where Mick bought two dim sims and two potato scallops from the hotbox and grabbed a chocolate milk from fridge. When he got to the counter, he also grabbed a Playboy magazine from below the shelf and placed it underneath his food. Mick's parents wouldn't approve of the magazine at his age, but Johno was fine with it – 'a part of life,' Johno believed.

They hit the road, in the septic truck, and Johno told Mick, 'We got a bit on today, so you ready for a big one?'

Mick nodded. 'Yeah, Johno, always … Hey, check out this new stuff.' He popped in the cassette tape, and the title track – 'Who Can It Be Now?' – started playing.

The sound of the brass horn reverberated within the truck cab, and Johno looked over at Mick in surprise, slightly raising his eyebrows and asking with an increased pitch in his tone at the end, 'Saxophone … *aye?*

Mick smiled at Johno as they drove out to a large older acreage property where the people were rather curious, mainly because nobody really knew them. The locals thought they were an inbred family, who had kids that rarely went to school and struggled with how to dress themselves properly. Mick always felt sorry for them, as he had no idea how to help people like that.

Johno and Mick needed to pump the septic tank of

this property, and as they drove there, they ate their food, listening to the cassette and enjoying the music.

Half an hour flew by, and Johno said, 'Let's quickly check the cricket score before we get out at this job, and then we can listen to the other side on the way to the next job.'

Mick ejected the tape and watched Johno's driving style. He had his left hand on the steering wheel and his right elbow nested on the door window, holding a cigarette between yellowing, orange-stained index and third fingers. Mick's internal belief was: *Why on earth would someone smoke? I'm certain girls wouldn't like it if you kissed them with that smoke smell.*

Johno tuned back into the radio and listened closely for an update of the score and laughed at the commentary style of Ritchie Benaud, while Mick was reading his Playboy magazine. On the front cover, there was a photo of that month's centrefold: Karen Price. Without wanting a response, Mick stated, 'This woman is amazing. Says here she wants to become a stunt woman. How cool!'

Johno watched the road as he changed down a gear, pumping the stiff clutch. The gears ground noisily, and he swore at the gearbox, 'Fuckin' get in second, ya bitch … Jeezus!'

Finally, they arrived at the mailbox of the property and entered the driveway, which snaked around the hill up to an old shanty-like house and shed. They pulled up near the underground septic tank. Johno had been there before, so he knew the location well. He turned the radio volume up so he could still hear the match.

They both jumped from their seat and sprang into action. When the pump was in place, Johno knocked on the door of the house. Nobody answered, so he started peeking through the windows and sneakily investigated the backyard for interesting things. Johno could hear the pump making a clogging noise and ran back to the truck, and competing with the radio volume, he yelled, 'You okay back there, Jerky?' He checked on Mick and then shut down the pump engine. 'Sounds like a blockage to me, bud. Grab the long pointy stick and run it up the hose.'

Johno assisted Mick to clear the blockage and complete the job. They then both jumped back in the truck and set off to their next location.

'No sign of the inbreds?' Mick asked Johno as he re-tuned the radio after it dropped out of reception. He then quickly requested, 'Hey, mate, can we put the tape back on? There's a song on the B-side I think you'll really like.'

'Yes, mate … besides, we're getting thumped at the cricket today anyway.'

Mick hit fast forward to the second track on the cassette: 'Be Good Johnny'.

Johno listened to the track, and as it played, he looked

over at Mick. 'Yeah, this is a good one. I reckon it's about you, Jerky.' He repeated lyrics with delay after hearing the words: '*Up to school you go, golden boy, always the dreamer out the school window, right?*'

Mick replied with a laugh and rebutted, 'It's literally got your name in the title, so it's obviously about you!"

'Good song,' Johno said. 'Funny track, but I like it.'

Mick was pleased and continued reading his Playboy magazine.

Johno asked him, 'Do you have plans for the weekend?'

Mick kept his head buried in the magazine and replied, 'Yeah, me and the other boys are heading out to the rodeo in Spud's car. Have you seen it? The orange Monaro.'

Johno looked over at Mick and said, 'No, not yet. Sounds like trouble, aye, Jerky? Have you got a plan yet for what to do after high school?'

Mick considered for a moment, then looked at Johno and said, 'Well, I'm sure as shit not hanging around here. Might join the army, like you did.'

Johno furrowed his brows and said, 'And end up with a wrecked back like I did? We'll have a chat about that another time, I reckon.' He made a mental note that he wouldn't sugar-coat the truth, to ensure that Mick fully understood that war heroes weren't all what was seen on the silver screen.

~

The following day, Johno had two water deliveries to make, one for Uncle Jack and one for the local vigneron, Tequil Le' Fur. Johno could never pronounce Tequil, so he took it upon himself to nickname him 'Tecca', or sometimes shortened it to just 'Tec'.

Tequil Le' Fur had lived in Brisbane for ten years before buying his stone house and putting in his vineyard, which was on the outskirts of town and bordered with Uncle Jack's cattle farm. He considered himself an outsider to the rest of the town, as he was tall and had a slender build, unlike the timber cutters or cattle men. He imagined his body was not built for slinging axes or wrestling calves. He was more refined and did things his way and not in line with the other locals – he refused to enter the pub, for it wasn't a place of 'his style'.

And by no means was he considered a high-volume producer, for his ten-acre plot rested on granite-based soil. The north-facing gradient gave great drainage with higher exposure to sunlight in winter when the sun dropped lower in the sky. His six acres of pinot gris were planted along the top, and the cabernet sauvignon ran parallel below; both varieties suited the humid conditions.

Depending on the rainfall and being able to avoid mould, his harvest could yield him over one hundred barrels of wine, which he sold to a South Australian connection through his family in the Barossa Valley. He was the only brother of four not to take up residence and settle in the state of South Australia when they all decided to move from France to Australia in search of discoveries in the 1960s.

While hiking the hills looking for new rocks to use for his house, Tequil noticed that the man Fred had warned him about – Cruickshanks – was 'snooping' around Uncle Jack's back paddock. Cruickshank was banging a white peg into the ground every twenty metres. For a time, Tequil sat and observed. He immediately worried that his neighbour, Jack, had already agreed to a deal with Sintex, which now looked to involve some mining operation, without consulting anyone else in the town.

Tequil wore a Jean-Antoine Lépine pocket watch on his hip that had been in his family for two generations. It sat below the bottom hemline of a brown swede vest on the right hip in a leather pouch, which attached to a well-worn leather belt with a plain, shiny silver belt buckle. He popped open the clip and looked at the white opal face – the Roman numerals showed 11.25 am. He had ordered a water delivery for midday and had a twenty-minute walk to get home.

Usually, Tequil would plan to be out when Johno arrived, but this time, he had something valuable that needed to be discussed with Johno.

Chapter Eleven

FRANK FINE

The *Country Life* newspaper was Frank's source of information about everything relating to the land. He also was quite fond of works by Henry Lawson, preferring Henry over Banjo for his directness and humour, which Frank appreciated and tried to mimic in his own life. But he never achieved the same jovial attributions, as Frank was firm and a significant character of a man.

He would always say to the folks who talked about movies, 'I never did like television much' – saying it the past tense – but he took a shine towards the animated Terrytoons cartoon series *Deputy Dawg*. Although he wasn't fond of television, he could justify that a five-minute cartoon was just enough to watch without getting distracted from reality.

Frank Fine carried a three blade 'old timer' pocket-knife kept length-ways inside an inbuilt leather case sewn to a well-worn brown leather belt with a shiny rectangular buckle, which had the letters WFF imbedded and gradually fell from left to right.

His ancestorial heritage wasn't well documented, but it was known that his grandfather's name was Wolfgang Fin, and originally, that side of the family was from the (then German) small town Lembach, which now was in France, and his wife Klara Baumann was from the German town Steinfeld. They met at school in Wissemburg in 1855 and married soon after high school.

At birth, Frank's parents named him Wolfgang Fredrich Fin, and he was born soon after they immigrated to Australia from Frankfurt, Germany. Before they arrived, both their families were farmers across Europe and heard of a new country where land was vast and able to be claimed or on a 'free-hold lease' without financial input if plans were in place to cultivate or clear for stock to graze upon.

Not long after they married, Wolfgang and Klara decided to break away from family tradition and find their own land to farm and moved to Australia in 1889. Frank's father, Heinrich, chose to name his son Wolfgang, but Frank took it upon himself to change his name on his first day of school, to avoid getting teased by other kids. Frank also added the 'e' to go from Fin to Fine, with hopes to anglicise it. This was the first thing that came to mind after he heard his parents talking about the German town of Frankfurt earlier that week.

Frank grew up to be a serious and stoic man, frugal with compliments and spoke few words, but when he did, they were not taken lightly. A phrase that stuck with Fred after Frank passed was, 'In order to cross the line, you first must know where the line is.'

Frank Fine owned a cattle farm, which he inherited from his family. It was along the stretch of highway where A Fine Motel now sat. The land was full of rough terrain that opened into flat grasslands with lantana flowering pink in springtime and creeping alongside winding creeks and entrapments, which were mostly dry, but they made the perfect spot for prickly pear cactus to grow. Frank would often carefully cut off a leaf with his pocketknife, to eat while he and Fred were out bush. It was a challenge to peel and eat without ending up with a thorn either in his hand while he peeled it or in his tongue when eating. 'They're not exactly flavoursome, but they don't taste bad,' he would remark, but the challenge made them even tastier, for some reason.

When Fred was six years old, his father took him hunting. Frank would not allow his family to eat the beef they produced on the farm, except at Christmas time. The beef cattle were farmed for the market, and that was how they made a crust. Instead, Frank would kill a wild wallaby, kangaroo, or deer, but never pigs, saying 'wild pigs are filth not fit for human consumption, but the yabbies love them'. They also made good bait for wild dog traps.

Fred wasn't certain what he enjoyed more about hunting: the scenery or spending time with his father. The kill, however, was never enjoyable, and the butchering even less so, but his mother's wallaby stew was always worth all the unpleasant smells and the gross sight of blood pooling like thickening bright red jelly on the ground next to the lifeless animal. Fred refused to eat raspberry jelly or Christmas trifle after that time, telling people that he wasn't a fan of the taste, and he kept the truth to himself.

One morning, both Frank and Fred got up early. The sun was still sleeping as they sat on the well-worn wooden step and tied their crusted leather bootlaces. They had been on hundreds of hunts together by this stage, and Fred knew the routine. Not a word was spoken, for they both knew silence was important during the hunt. They set off to the back corner of the property where the big dam was and where the native wildlife would gather. They passed through the flats, ignoring an iguana that rustled through the grass and climbed up an old scribbly gum tree.

Frank noticed a wallaby raise its head in their direction as it grazed on grass intended only for Frank's cattle. The dew sparkled on its white chest fur, and in the distance, the sun peaked over the rough-ridged mountain tops. The sleepy old wallaby did not see the pair quietly crawling on their stomachs to get into place, laying on top of a red granite mound, readying themselves to make the shot.

Fred looked at the cuteness of the wallaby and smiled at the beauty of the land and the peaceful fleeting moment the three of them had together. He then cupped his hands over his ears as his father raised the rifle to his shoulder and looked down the iron sights of the barrel while he steadied himself.

Taking a deep breath, Frank whispered, 'You will not die in vain,' and pulled the trigger. Frank's 303-rifle gave a hard kick, felt in Frank's shoulder as the projectile fell on target. They both heard a thump directly after the gunshot, followed by crackling echoes through the hills.

'Good shot, Dad,' whispered Fred.

'We got him,' remarked Frank.

For as long as Fred could remember, his dad had the same routine and wore the same clothes, and he was always accompanied by a farm dog. Multiple farm dogs came and went, with the average life span of a farm dog being approximately three years before they died from either a blue tick or a snake bite. Frank's dogs were all blue heelers – cattle dogs – and they were all named Deputy. Frank loved naming his dog's Deputy, because in his mind, he was the Sheriff.

Deputy number one was a great dog. She would rip the head off a snake before you'd even know it was behind you. She must have killed a hundred snakes in her life, but her last was too much to bounce back from. Fred and Beryl were playing rugby league one day after school, kicking the ball when it rolled over the fence into the long grass.

Beryl ran over to retrieve the ball and stepped on a red-bellied black snake laying in the long brown grass, which bit her multiple times on both legs. Deputy was only just behind her and grabbed the snake by the belly, vigorously shaking it from side to side like a baby shakes a rattle, breaking different sections of the snake's spine. However, Deputy was bitten on the neck and chest.

Fred ran quickly inside to grab the 410-shotgun hidden behind the laundry door with bullets on the exposed stud bearing above the door, and then he called for help. Deputy waited by Beryl's side, panting heavily. Beryl was surprisingly calm, and Fred was proud of her for not panicking. She was possibly in shock as Fred passed the gun to Frank, having just finished loading it, and they briskly walked through the yard, looking for the snake.

Beryl called, 'I think it's over there,' pointing to the long grass to her right.

Frank spied the snake and made one direct shot to the snake's head, and then he picked up Beryl and rushed her over to the car, with Deputy running close behind. Frank sped in his FJ Holden Ute for the forty-kilometre journey to the nearest hospital in the neighbouring town, with Deputy laying across Frank's lap.

While Fred was in the waiting area of the hospital,

he noticed Deputy walking with a semi-sideways wobble. Fred asked Deputy to 'hang in there'.

Frank walked out and told Fred to take the ute back to his mother's work and tell her what had happened, while he waited in the hospital with Beryl.

Fred was worried about Deputy as well.

Frank explained, 'Mate, she's a working dog, you don't need to worry about her.' He gave Fred a quick rehash on how to change gears in the ute, ending the conversation with, 'Son, do as I say, and everything will be just fine.'

Fred drove the long dusty road to his mother's shop, doing his best to dodge potholes and the thick corrugated run-offs in the road, all the while sitting on a rolled-up towel for extra height so he could see over the dash. He made it to Pearl's shop and rushed into the grocery store to inform his mother of the afternoon's crisis. They both then headed back to the hospital.

When they arrived, Frank met them in the hallway and explained, 'Beryl has some kind of paralysis and is unable to walk.' He told them that the doctor wasn't sure how long it would take for her to regain the use of her legs.

Fred noticed the blue hospital initials embroidered onto a pillowcase placed over Deputy, who lay silently with her head nestled between her front paws and her back legs tucked under her body. He walked over to comfort her but observed that her stomach wasn't moving like it usually did.

Frank bent a knee and lowered his head to match Fred's height and said, 'I'm sorry, son, she's gone. That red-bellied snake got her good, but she saved your sister's life. She was a great dog and did her job well to the end.

Fred did his best, but nothing could help the tears from trickling down his cheek.

Frank suggested, 'You can pick the perfect spot in the backyard for us to bury her, if you like?'

Fred looked down at the pillowcase. 'She always liked sitting under Mum's lilli pilli tree'. He remembered sitting under it with Beryl, peeling the purple berries to eat, Deputy continually trying to eat them, but the bitterness mustn't have been to her taste.

Beryl returned from hospital after a few days, but she permanently lost the use of her legs and was confined to a wheelchair ever since. It wasn't too long before they heard of a farmer down the road with a litter of blue heeler pups, and Deputy, the second, was chosen.

Chapter Twelve

JESSIE

June 1981

The veranda was a cold place to sleep for most, but Jessie never opposed or seemed to mind at all, except for her first winter – those two cold months of June and July, Fred let her into his room to sleep, and she'd sneak up onto his bed.

One of the natural cane armchairs at top of the veranda stairs was her observation post, and from there she was able to spot any foreigner meandering by and watch their movements closely, with her uniquely asymmetrical-coloured eyes: left one white and right one blue. Her coat was grey across the front and over her rear quarter legs, and she had a thick white belt around her belly, separating her black-speckled hip junctions and connecting to a white shield shape on her chest that was like the protective collar a pig dog would wear.

The sun wouldn't wake her in the early morning hours, as she slept in a curled position with her nose buried under either leg pit, until the creaking and cracking of footsteps on internal floorboards made her ears prick and flicker.

Fred had picked her up from the butcher Jed Moreton at the start of the new year. Jed's faithful blue heeler bitch had pups, and everyone knew the bloodline was good from his dogs. Fred and Johno examined the options around the back of the Eat Moreton Meat butcher shop.

Jed had taken them through the shop and led them past the coolrooms to behind the shop. 'Easy girl,' he said as he lifted then pulled open the heavy wooden door that was hanging by just one top hinge of the re-purposed thunderbox. He then let the men inside to look at his litter of blue heeler pups.

'They all look pretty much the same,' said Johno.

Fred looked at the pups entwined around their mother and counted five. He went to say, 'I thought you said there were six, Jed?' but cut himself short when he spotted a black- and grey-freckled tail poking out of an empty tin of dog food. He pulled the pup out and held it by the back of the neck; it was so young, its eyes were still sealed shut.

'You found the runt, I see, funny eyes on it,' stated Jed.

'This little lady looks just fine, if you ask me. I'll be back in six or seven weeks, mate,' said Fred.

Jed smiled, exposing his missing left canine tooth.

'Too easy, Fred. And before you guys go, I'll give you a sample of my latest creation for the next sausage competition. I'm using camel meat for these ones, so let me know what you think.'

When Jessie was old enough, Fred picked her up, and over the following months, Jessie grew to love Monday mornings. She could sense the beginning of a new week when Fred got up a tiny bit earlier to head to Arthur's Bakery with Johno for the ritualistic pie, and Fred would buy new eggs for the week. She was eager to go with him, knowing full well Margaret was a pushover for pastry. With her tongue hanging out and trailing Fred's heels closely, Jessie maintained her manners, daring not to chase any street chickens they came upon, with anticipation of her treat. She also remembered the punishment dealt by Fred the first and last time she caught one and brought it home – she vowed never to do that again.

Jessie's loyalty towards Fred grew with every ball thrown for her to fetch or bone left for her to bury, and she even loved it when Fred pretended to throw the ball but hide it behind his back, smirking at her with a suggestive 'come on, then' look on his face. Her favourite meal was the leftovers at dinner time after dark, which provided a variety of surprises, compared with the dry biscuits she received most mornings. She loved Beryl almost just as much, thinking *she sits at the perfect height for pats and scratches behind the ears.*

And today, while she was sitting upon her veranda armchair, she eyed the new miner's vehicle arrive at the motel car park. *I don't like to look of this white round-legged rider, it's a lot cleaner than Fred's rider and all the other ones around town*, she thought. *And its owner smells different to the rest of my friends, similar to those colourful blob things that hang on the end of the thin, sharp, spiky plants along the front garden fence* – referring to the rose bushes Pearl planted in winters past. Her suspicious eyes gleamed at the man that got out of the car, following him closely as he locked the vehicle and entered the main doorway to collect his room key.

Her protective nature was so strong it went well further than the average dog, well beyond her house yard, owner and street, and it was more in line with that of a wolf taking the entire town and surrounding properties as her territory.

Fred had Jessie 'fixed up' after her first litter of pups. That way, when she wandered out to play for her nightly roam through one of her escape hatches, she had no chance of having any more offspring. On her midnight runs, she looked for anything 'out of the ordinary' and not belonging in her town.

Fred admired this trait, as it was something he felt akin to and envied her ability to roam freely. Although, he did worry from time to time, especially when her return was not before sun-up. Like the time she stayed out, gone for over forty-eight hours and not having come home for supper. He swung by next door to talk to Johno. 'Mate, I got a feeling I know where she is, so do you want to come for a look for her with me?'

Johno quickly agreed, saying, 'Yep, just let me drop the weight of the carjack.' Johno had been doing a service on his four-wheel drive, and his face was covered in break dust.

They drove out to the north-west side of the town, to where the old dump was.

Fred said, 'She's had a thing for that place lately. I've had to wash her three times in the last week after she comes back from one of her runs.'

They arrived at the dump and slowly drove through to assess the different areas and piles or rubbish.

'They must have burnt lately; it doesn't smell as rotten as usual,' said Johno.

Fred was quiet, just squinting into the last hours of sunlight before dark set. He stopped the car and turned off the engine. His ears were ringing, but he could hear an intermittent squeaking behind the pile of metals. 'Do you hear that?' he asked.

'I hear something,' replied Johno.

They both opened their doors and walked over towards where the sounds were coming from. When they got close enough, they could see Jessie bending down with her front paws, trying to remove an empty tin of baked beans from her snout. She'd been scrounging for food when trying to lick the bottom of an empty can of baked beans that had been pushed so hard against her nose it covered her eyes and stuck to her face, blinding her and making her unable to open her mouth to bark for help.

'Bloody hell, girl, what have you done to yourself?' Fred asked.

Feeling embarrassed, she had nothing to say to him but give a tiny whimper.

Johno broke the silence on her behalf, saying, 'Bit hungry, hey girl? Isn't your owner feeding you enough?' He scowled at Fred before he continued, 'I'll hold her around the chest, and you remove the tin.' Johno kneeled to his left side and held her tight while Fred slowly twisted the tin can off her nose, trying his best not to cut her skin any more than it was already damaged.

'Jeezus, girl, you're lucky we came looking when we did … not sure how much longer you would have lasted.'

Johno figured, 'Bet she's never been happier seeing you, aye, mate.' And he gave her a rough scratch above the tail.

'Right,' said Fred, 'let's get you home.'

Jessie did a little turn and jumped in the car. Feeling embarrassed, and yet again hungry, she sat quietly between them as they drove home, thinking *dry biscuits and leftovers are a better option for me, moving forward.*

Chapter Thirteen

PEARL FINE

Pearl had never been a suspicious person; she took things at face value and relied on a trust built within her community. But when Sintex began asking questions about certain property owners and how receptive the locals were to change, her snake senses engaged.

Yes, she was a progressive, but in her own way; Pearl certainly didn't want to upset the balance of the bush for any corporation trying to increase their bottom line. What Pearl particularly disliked was gossip, and possibly to some detriment of the town, her suspicions as to Sintex's 'plans' lay dormant, deciding not to add discussions to the usual rumour mill around town.

What Pearl enjoyed the most was writing poetry, painting with oils, and listening to jazz records, especially when she was cooking. Her chestnut upright piano sat in the corner of the living room close to the Singer sewing machine she got from her mother, which was no longer in use. The piano, however, would barely have time to gather dust between the keys, with either her or Beryl playing it. Pearl always played a walking bass line with her left hand and a bluesy jazz melody with her right.

She mostly wore her hair in a short brown bob or in the same way her much-loved movie star – Audrey Hepburn – did in her films. Floral dresses were her favourite, with days or weeks between the use of eyeliner, foundation, or any makeup, for that matter. 'She didn't need to wear it,' Frank would often remark.

While Pearl liked all kinds of music, she loved jazz the most, especially by the Duke – Duke Ellington – and that song he did with Juan Tizol, 'Caravan', was on high rotation on the family record player. She loved the way the melody drifted over the 6/8 feel-drum and bassline rhythm, which made it sound like a distant. world to her, and she wished to explore it in the same way Fred felt the need to leave town when he was young.

Beryl loved the way her mother described the jazz ensemble, saying, 'The band and their instruments remind me of the genetic makeup of a person.' She'd then go on to say, 'You can imagine that the drummer would be the skeletal system, providing weight, pace and feel. The double bass is the muscles, with strength binding everything together, helping form structure and shape the link, with the chordal instruments – like guitar and piano, which both play a role similar to the body's organs – pumping colour and tone, just the same as skin holding everything together, giving reason or perspective.'

Beryl would interject with, 'Mum, skin's not an organ, is it?"

'Yes, it is B, but before we move on, we can't forget melody, the pretty frills of a vocalist and melodic instruments … like brass would be what?'

There would only be a few moments of silence before Beryl would pipe up with, '*Hair*?'

'Yes!' Pearl would then go on to say, 'The hair, the clothes, the shoes, makeup, all help enhance and embrace the beauty of everything, working together as a team, playing their role behind it.'

Beryl would let this information sink in before giving a calculated response. 'Sounds like a family to me, Mum.' She always surprised her mother, and Pearl felt proud, believing it a profound conclusion for a girl aged six.

Pearl grew up in the Brisbane suburb of Morningside, and as she got older, she often recalled times when they had in-class drill practice in her primary school years in the event of a bombing during World War Two, so they could be prepared for an attack. Pearl would say, 'The principle sounded the sir and we'd all jump under our desks, place wooden clothes peg in our mouths to bite down on to prevent our teeth from shattering, but also so we wouldn't scream and alert any enemy foot soldiers where we were. When you think about it, if a bomb hit, we'd all be dead anyway, wouldn't we?' And she'd chuckle about how silly the scenario seemed. 'At night-time, we had to put sheets over the windows to black out the lights, so enemy planes that flew overhead wouldn't see the houses below. They even covered car headlights when they drove at night. It was a scary time to be a kid.'

When Pearl was grocery shopping one day at the local four square, where she also worked, she saw the owner's children playing with kittens in the house yard next to the store. Pearl approached the children and inquired if the kittens happened to be for sale.

When she arrived home that afternoon, to Fred and Beryl's great surprise, they became the owners of a cute and cuddly black cat. Fred asked if it had a name, and Pearl replied, 'Not yet, darling. What would you like to call him?'

Fred, six years of age at the time, looked around the room and saw the Thelonious Monk album *Straight No Chaser* standing against the wall by the record player. 'How about Thelonious Monk, Mum?'

Beryl quickly interrupted with, 'I can't even say Theolony Monk, so how about we call him Theo for short?'

'Yes, that's a lovely name!' Pearl replied.

Behind the houses of Harveston were the old outdoor toilets, commonly referred to as the 'thunder box' or 'dunny', which had now mostly been turned into garden sheds or storage of some kind after the government brought in sewage channels and septic tanks to all country towns.

Pearl loved politics, and especially the work of former Prime Minister, Gough Whitlam, for the town's sewerage and plumbing. Fred remembered his mum saying, 'The best Prime Minister by far has been Gough,' and how she objected with how his ousting occurred, but she also sited that his undoing was, 'Too much action, too quickly for the population and opposing party to come to terms with.'

Apart from Frank's death, she would write to Fred saying, 'The hardest thing to live through was State Premier Sir Joh Bjelke-Petersen's fascist political ideals and hillbilly dictating style of governing.'

Pearl also loved nature and the magic of the night sky. She would take the kids out once it was dark enough, lay out a thick woollen blanket and tell them tales and stories of the constellations and how they related to one another. Incorporating Greek mythology and the Aboriginal Dreamtime stories she knew, Pearl was able to point out Orion, the Big Dipper, the Crab, and the Scorpion.

Fred loved to joke and ask if there was a yabby in the sky to boil in the Big Dipper? Pearl always replied, 'I'm not sure, son, but there are some in the dam out back. If you and Beryl would like to catch some tomorrow, I can boil them up for dinner for us.'

Fred found great joy in yabbying, all he needed was a

bucket, a piece of string and some cut-up bits of meat left over from his dad's latest kill, or anything Deputy was yet to take and bury in her secret spot. As kids, he and Johno would go down to the dam at the back of the property – the one with the most yabbies was farthest away and the best, because no other kids knew how to get to it. They would sit on the banks of the dam for hours, trying to see who could land the biggest catch and which of them could skim rocks the best. Johno would take the single-shot 22-calibre Winchester bolt action. It wasn't a pretty thing, but it did the job in case they came across any pests – at least then they could help Frank by killing a fox or a snake.

After they filled the bucket with yabbies, they would take off, racing home for Pearl to cook them. 'The trick is to add lots of salt to the water,' Pearl said. 'And when you think you've added enough, add another half a handful.' Pearl loved cooking so much that she would enter her cooking in competitions and shows across the neighbouring towns, with her 'piece de resistance' being the 'wallaby and venison with fennel seed and Cumberland-style sausage'. This was a fat snag and had to be cooked in an oven to make sure the juices remained inside, and it was consistently cooked through without drying out or burning one side.

The other thing Pearl made so well were scones. Most people would think scones were just scones, but not Pearl's scones. She added a pinch of cinnamon with her butternut pumpkin and potato scones, using lemonade as the liquid to the mix, which made them stand apart from the rest. Pearl acquired her cooking skills from her mother, but she also worked in a mixed European-Australian restaurant in Brisbane on weekends while she attended high school, where she gained experience cooking meat on an open fire. The money she earnt helped her parents make the mortgage repayments on their house, without having to sell, due to the Great Depression.

There was one time of year Fred and Beryl especially looked forward to her cooking speciality, as she made the best Christmas plum pudding. Her secret recipe had been cultivated over decades by grannies before her and passed down along the way.

(Granny Cavanagh)   This one I make
                    Xmas Plum Pudding (Good)
2 Cups S.R. Flour, 1 cup sugar 1½ ptt mixed
Fruit (1 cup cold water with 1 heaped teaspoon
Bi-Carb-Soda dissolved in it) 1 cup Boiling
water with 1 dessertspoon butter melted in it.
Vanilla & Rum. Mix flour-sugar- Fruit
Cherries- nuts- Spices, then add Butter mixture
the cold water -soda mixture Dip cloth
into hot water- sprinkle with P Flour. Put
mixture into it- tie leaving room to swell
boil 3 hours

After Frank passed away, Pearl and the kids would often tell fun stories about him, and the most popular one Pearl would recall was when Frank lost his left index finger in the mincer while making venison and beef sausages.

Whenever this story was told, Beryl couldn't contain herself, butting in halfway through the story and belting out with laughter, saying, 'And Deputy pounced at the ground and ate his finger faster than Dad could yell at her to "DROP IT, YA BITCH!"'

Fred would add how his dad said, 'It was lucky he was right-handed and didn't lose his trigger finger!'

Pearl was a caring, salt of the earth woman, and she was both admired and respected within the community. She volunteered with the girl local guides and Country Women's Association (CWA), where they made sandwiches for the firefighters during bushfire seasons and other emergencies, such as the 1974 floods, which left communities disconnected without food, water, power, or communication.

To Fred, the motel was all that was left of his mother, and he knew that the conviction Pearl had inside her needed to be carried forward to keep her memory alive. All Fred needed to figure out was how he could do it in his own way and what was best for Harveston. And he knew deep down that there was no way his mother would ever have approved of a mining company walking in and taking over.

Chapter Fourteen

THE JERKY BOYS

May 1971, Part One

It was May 1971, and Mick, Biddy, Timmo and Spud had just walked about thirty minutes along a snigging track Mick's dad had been using lately to drag logs; the earth had been turned over, and the smell of fresh soil was in the air.

Mick constantly surveyed the surrounding areas as they looked for suitable trees and material to make sure they would have the prime spot to build his next cubby. 'Not here, a bit further, I reckon,' said Mick.

About halfway to the spot, Spud found shade then stopped in the middle of the track and removed a pack of Camel cigarettes from his back trouser pocket and then felt his other pockets for a cigarette lighter, finding it in the front pocket. He held the lighter to his face and squinted his eyes when the flame hit the paper and smoke first appeared.

The boys stared at the red cherry on the end of Spud's cigarette as he blew a smoke ring up into the sky. Spud was always pinching smokes off his dad, so when Timmo blurted, 'Friggin' hell, where did you get them,' no one was surprised with the answer.

'I've got eleven left. So, three each, unless someone doesn't want one?' Then he handed them each a smoke while they stood in the cool thick shade of a camphor laurel tree for ten minutes.

When Spud climbed up the first two branches of the tree, Timmo placed the water bottle on the ground and dropped the shovel to light his smoke up. He noticed the cobbler's pegs had started to gather in Spud's socks and then looked to see that everyone's socks were just the same after they'd walked in some weeded grass.

'Aye, Biddy, where's Darcy playing footy this weekend?' asked Mick as he kicked a lump of dirt, sending rocks and dust into the air. Darcy was a few years older than the boys and one of the best young footballers that came from town in recent years.

'I think he's playing the Clydesdales at their home ground this afternoon. Dad's taken him over.'

They continued down the trail and made it to the spot Mick planned to use. The area was used by his dad to store the logs ready for transport to the timber mill a few towns away. Mick's parents had inherited the land, owning it for the past thirty years. It was near a one-thousand-hectare block of rugged mountain countryside to the north of Harveston, and his dad selectively cleared it to maintain a steady income with the sale of hardwood eucalyptus trees.

In recent years, sales were slow, and money was tight. The land had been in their name for generations, but when Sintex made an offer and bought them out, only to lease the house and land back to them to live on and work, it was something Mick's parents couldn't turn down.

Most days, an orange and white Stihl chainsaw swung by Mick's dad, Colin, and it was the only thing heard breaking the silence between the boys chattering and the sound of the bush as they played in the dirt patches and ground was cleared in the wake of a bulldozer snig trail or turn spot.

The other three boys all lived on house blocks in town, and unlike Mick, they rarely had cobbler's pegs clinging to their socks but enjoyed what went with it just as much as he did. Mick's parents' land was the main place the boys played on school break and some weekends, and with the freedom they aligned with what 'adult life would be like'.

They sat down for a drink break, and then Mick started to lay down the ins and outs of cubby building.

'When selecting material to build the ultimate cubby house,' Mick said, 'we need to find the best qualities that will provide insulation, strength, and shelter from the sun and rain. Otherwise, it's just not worth our time.'

The three of them sat on a log as Mick stood in front and outlined the details of the task at hand, drawing a sketch in the dirt of what he wanted. 'Oh … and watch out for black or brown snakes and red-back spiders that live under the bark.' He looked at them intensely, stating, 'Snakes are everywhere here, and they like hiding under logs in the cool, away from the sun.'

Spud piped up, 'I heard that if you get bit by a black snake, you need to stop the venom from entering the body's bloodstream as fast as possible or you can die before making it to hospital.'

Mick was almost eight years old, and he had no clue that only three generations before him, not long after World War One, his forebears were building the same structures, though not as a playhouse but a place to lay their head after a day cutting timber in the bush. Mick was from a bloodline that predominantly worked with their hands on the land either via farming or logging timber. 'Stringybark is the best for walls, as it's dense enough for protection and malleable enough to work with. Paperbark would be better, but we don't have much around this area,' he explained.

They had no tools (apart from a tomahawk and a shovel) to cut and shape walls, so this was a valuable consideration.

They selected small trees with similar diameters to their own legs for the outer poles – ones they could cut down with the axe, which gave way without too much fight.

It was Timmo's turn on the axe. He was on his own, working about twenty metres from the others, cutting away at the small tree while Mick, Biddy and Spud were messing around and collecting bark from a nearby log and playing cricket with the shovel and lumps of hard dirt. Mick's dad had fallen the logs over the past few months, and they were the size of telephone poles. They had been laying on the ground long enough for the bark to begin to detach from its hardwood surface. The walls of the cubby had now been built up enough so as to make a start on the roof.

Timmo was definitely working up a sweat, swinging away at the tree in the hot sun, and he walked over to their makeshift 'supply area' where they left the snack bag and water. He looked down at the plastic Cottee's cordial bottle repurposed for water only and sat down in front of the log pile. He placed the axe head on the ground to his right and lent the handle against the stump, which he sat on, resting his legs. He then quenched his thirst by taking a long gulp of the water. He could taste the remnants of a sweet orange flavour around the lip of the bottle, but the water was what his dry mouth needed.

Biddy and Spud walked over to join him, as they felt the same weariness in the heat of the mid-morning sun. As they approached Timmo, Biddy stopped talking to Spud and stood still, looking as if he'd seen a ghost.

Spud turned to him and then to Timmo and yelled, 'Shit, snake!' pointing his finger towards Timmo's left side.

Timmo looked around and was instantly struck on the tips of his fourth and fifth fingers on his left hand by the snake's razor-sharp bite before he had time to jump. He then quickly picked up the axe, but the snake was faster than lightning through a drainpipe, darting off before Timmo could lift it to make a swing.

Mick had heard the commotion and came running over from the log to see Timmo turn towards the stump he'd been sitting on and place his left hand down flat with his palm up.

Spud and Biddy stood still in shock as Mick jogged over.

They then watched Timmo lift the tomahawk axe above his head and strike the first row of knuckles behind the bite mark of the snake.

'FRIGGIN HELL, TIMMO!' yelled Mick as they all watched the brightest pinkish-red blood any of the boys had seen spurting out from Timmo's hand, and then his two fingers rolled off the stump onto the powdery dirt.

Timmo dropped the axe and gripped his left hand tight with his right to contain the bleeding.

They were at least an hour walk from Mick's house, which meant if they ran, this time could be reduced to forty minutes.

'I'll run back and get Dad's ute and then come back. You guys stay here,' Spud said.

Mick replied, 'I'm a better driver than you, so I'll come, and Biddy can wait here with Timmo.'

It was decided without contention, and the two set off to get the rescue vehicle.

At the time of the unexpected amputation, due to being partly in shock, none of the boys questioned Timmo's reasoning behind the sudden decision to chop off two of his own fingers.

Mick and Spud raced back as fast as they could.

'Hey, Spud, did you get a good look at that snake?'

'Yeah, I did.'

'Well, what was it?'

Spud gave a long pause, huffing and puffing.

Mick knew he was trying to catch his breath.

'Well, it wasn't a black or a brown snake.'

'Okay, what was it?' Mick asked.

'I only know this because we had one in the back shed last week. It was just a dirty scrub py*thon*,' Spud said with a raised tone.

Mick almost laughed. 'Do you think we should tell Timmo it was harmless?'

'Ha, maybe not today, I reckon,' said Spud.

It was at least two years before any of the boys let Timmo know the truth.

Timmo's only response when he found out was, 'Frig off! You guys are full of shit.'

Chapter Fifteen

BERYL FINE

'Impossibility exists only in the mind of the pessimist.'

It was September 1959, and Beryl sat at the piano and let the sentence sink in. Her mother had started teaching her how to play two octave arpeggio pattens; however, her right hand resembled a pretzel and lacked the poise and grace that Pearl had achieved.

'Okay, Mum, I'll keep working on it.'

'I'll be in the backyard if you need help.'

Beryl's ability to focus was that of a starving dog with a bone, unable to think of anything else or sway between two subjects. This was a strength with her musical talents and a weakness when it came time to move on to another topic.

She was fond of her mother's ability to play the piano, and although she couldn't get her fingers to run up and down scales like Pearl could, nothing stopped her from giving it a go. Beryl practised on the piano before and after school. She would listen to the same songs her mum liked and learnt quickly how to place the vinyl on the record player without making that terrible scratching sound she hated so much, often calling out to Mum, 'Which record is "Goodbye Porkpie Hat" on?'

Pearl would call back from the kitchen, '*Mingus Ah Um*, sweetie,'

'*Ah Um*? Okay, Mum, thanks.' Even at an early age, Beryl grasped the deep sadness and what she felt was oppression oozing from the instruments with every note. The bond between Beryl and 'Goodbye Porkpie Hat' became even stronger after the loss of her legs, and when she realised the power of the song after finding out that it was a tribute to the late famous jazz tenor saxophonist Lester Young, and how she compared it to the loss of her legs.

Beryl listened closely to the musical notes of each instrument and tried to imitate them on the upright chestnut piano. When she was younger and still had her legs to run around on, she couldn't hit the right notes and made a lot of mistakes. She couldn't even reach the pedals, but using her ears, she found a way to lock in time with the rhythms.

Pearl and Beryl loved this time together, while Fred and Frank were out tending to cattle or hunting. It allowed them to spend quality time bonding over their shared love for music. Pearl proudly remarked, 'If jazz were a person, it would be just like Beryl. Always up for an adventure and never one to shy away from a challenge.'

Beryl was strong-willed and wouldn't back down when something stood in her way. When she grew older, Beryl, forever the grand optimist, often felt somewhat glad it was her that got bitten by that snake and not Fred, saying, 'Fred wouldn't last a week in a wheelchair, he'd go mad being stuck in this chair, unable to keep his mind in check with his body.'

For Beryl, the years that passed post-snake bite were challenging not only physically but mentally difficult to wade through. Being picked on at school due to her differences was one thing, but not being able to participate in sports and outdoor activities was another. And as a teenager, the idea of ever trying to pair up with a boyfriend was unfathomable. She did have a crush on Fred's mate Johno for a while. She thought he was smart, and he loved music (though not her kind of music, but he still listened). He was also funny, brave, strong, good at sport – especially footy – and he always stuck up for her and tried to include her in anything he and the other boys were doing.

However, that candle extinguished before it had a chance to glow, when Johno left for Kapooka with Fred. And then, Beryl buried her head in books, loving fantasy stories of strange worlds and faraway places as a form of escapism. And in the real world, she put all her focus into the one thing that never said no to her or told her that she couldn't do something or made fun of her. Her ears became her strength, and the piano her power.

Sometime after the snake bite, Frank realised that he needed to engineer a new sitting style for Beryl as she sat at the piano. He spent time sitting and watching her play, pretending to read the paper, and then he started to develop an idea for a lever-type of stick, or a tool that would rest on the pedal then under her left forearm. Frank figured that the left forearm would be better suited to control the pedals, due to it being more stationary in position when playing rhythm, or a walking baseline would allow her right arm to freely move up and down on the upper end of the ivory and ebony keys.

Frank worked in the shed for a week, without Beryl's knowledge of his plan, and he fiddled with the prototype of the prosthetic-style arm, fashioned with a strap made from an old belt, to fix it to the forearm.

Pearl and Fred knew what he was doing and kept Frank's creation a secret as well.

After Frank had finished making the new pedal arm for Beryl, he wrapped it up in a soft leather sheath. Beryl opened it when she got home from school and at first was perplexed. She then sat down at the piano, and Frank positioned the pedal so she could give it a go.

Before too long, she got used to it, and for the first time since losing her legs, she could make and hear the sustained notes and chords. Her eyes lit up and cheeks glowed with happiness. She was lost for words and squeezed Frank tight with an emotional hug and a simple, 'Thanks, Dad.'

Chapter Sixteen

DJANGO REINHARDT

May 1971, Part Two

The ground shuddered behind Siskas.

She was twelve years old and ran as fast as her legs could carry her.

Biskas had received his Qwasarm at thirteen years of age, and now at fourteen, he had not found the need to use his weapon yet. He wasn't too far behind. His left leg had been injured when it was stuck between moss rock and lamp log just one moon before.

Liskas was at the rear, holding off the shadow creeper with his giant reflective shield. He had swung his Qwasarm in many battles before now, but this time it remained in its sheath.

The creeper was quick in the dark, but when hit by light, it would retreat into the nearest burrow hole, cave, or crevasse from whence it came.

Liskas held his shield tight, angling the shiny bright beams of day's end sunlight directly at the body of the shadow creeper.

'Beryl, I'm heading to the shops before they close for groceries,' Pearl said one afternoon.

Beryl took no notice; her head had been stuck in her latest book: *Kingdom of Kane*. And she read on:

The three of them had been foraging in the field for fruit and fungi for the last four humbs, until the sun started to fall. The fruit was partly for food, but when the juices of a Casuuna berry were combined with the stork of the mallytoad mushroom and sweet juice apple, it would create the perfect paste to apply directly to an open wound.

Pearl walked over to her. 'Beryl, it's three o'clock, I'll be gone for an hour, okay?'

Without adverting her eyes from the book, Beryl replied, 'Yes, Mum.' And then she continued to read:

He knew Siskas and Biskas could make it to the portal if he held the creeper back for just a couple of tucks longer. He looked at the sun hanging low in the sky and yelled, 'How much longer?'
Biskas called back, 'Just one more tuck, I think.'

Biskas had caught up to Siskas by now and was clenching his teeth and ignoring the pain.

They were both getting closer to the mud portal before it sealed shut, trapping them in the rainforest, which at night turned rotten.

The three of them now lived in the region known only as Sunken Earth. This region formed after a dozen tsunami waves hit the coastline of their old region home in the rainforest. Sunken Earth was deep underground and could only be accessed through a water channel that linked up to a major mud portal.

With her head buried in the pages, another hour or more passed by before she placed her thin silver steel bookmark in the book and popped the book into the left-side pouch of her wheelchair. She looked out the window; it was almost sunset, and her music student was late for their weekly appointment.

Timmo was usually quite punctual and came to Beryl's house for music theory lessons. She couldn't teach him piano; he had no interest in it. His love was for the big loud punchy sounds a saxophone could produce. Beryl also couldn't teach him how to improve his embouchure, he would have to learn this for himself, as no brass teachers lived within fifty miles, or so she believed. She looked at the clock, then picked up her book again.

A familiar car rolled into the driveway, and the

engine was turned off. Beryl confirmed it by ear: it was her mother returning. Then she heard the squeak of the door opening before it shut with a *clud*. The wedge-heel footsteps walked quicker than normal along the wooden floorboards, which sounded her mother's approach; she carried the groceries and the latest news heard while at the shops.

'Your student didn't arrive, did he?'

'Tim, no, he didn't … but how do you know?'

Pearl talked as she walked into the kitchen, and Beryl wheeled closely behind. 'I was at the shops; old Mrs Hooper was there getting bread, oh, apparently Sintex have been pestering her as well and trying to buy her out, but that's another story … Anyway, she'd just been to the butcher. Mr Moreton's son, Spud, was out with Tim when he accidently chopped his fingers off.'

'He *what?*'

'Apparently, a snake bit him on the fingers, and he just chopped them off, or something.'

Beryl's eyebrows raised in disbelief.

And it'd been so long since Beryl's snake bite that Pearl had all but forgotten how she ended up in a wheelchair.

Over at Timmo's house, Timmo lay on his side, his right arm tucked under his head, his bandaged left hand resting on his hip. He couldn't help but look up at the sparkling brass saxophone resting on the shelf, and realising it was not possible to play a full scale with two less fingers, he rolled over on his back, shut his eyes and tried to sleep.

A few weeks later, urged by his parents to return to his lessons, Timmo walked across the oval where a known magpie nested and heard the shriek of the black and white bastard. He turned and saw the bird aiming its beady eyes and pointed beak in his direction.

It had been one month since his 'accident', and his parents pushed him to get back to his life. He started jogging backwards to keep his eyes locked with the pesky bird, ducking his head down to avoid a swift peck to the noggin', while at the same time, he waved a snapped eucalyptus branch up to startle the maggie as he ran further outside its territory.

Once he was out of range, he stopped and yelled, 'I wasn't doing anything to you!'

The maggie watched and flew back to its nest and let out a shriek – *kaarrr, kaarrr* – as if it won that battle.

Trotting the rest of the way, he arrived at his music lesson, leaving his instrument behind for the first time. He hadn't had a lesson for weeks, and this was the first time he and Beryl could discuss what they were going to do now, given that he had less fingers.

She fell silent on the incident itself and chose not to

ask anything of the event, only saying, 'Has this changed your feelings towards music?'

Timmo frowned and replied, 'Ahh, no, but I can't play anymore.'

'Can't play sax, you mean,' Beryl advised him. And then she said, 'Have you heard of the guitarist Django Rienhardt?

Timmo shook his head. 'No, I haven't.'

Beryl explained, 'He was a gypsy jazz guitarist, who at the age of eighteen in 1928, lost his fingers in a fire. I believe he was living in a caravan or a wagon when a candle was knocked over and a fire burnt it down. He almost lost his leg as well, but he adapted, gave up the banjo and violin and learnt how to hold a guitar. He then became one of the most well-known and loved jazz guitarists in the world.'

Timmo looked to her with interest.

'Still,' she affirmed, 'he played with Coleman Hawkins and Benny Carter, even the Duke, I think.' She wheeled over to the record collection and found the vinyl album and gave it to Timmo. 'Listen, think on it, and remember: impossibility exists only in the mind of the pessimist. Now, I'll let you in on a secret – I've been trying out writing my own jazz songs for the past few years and never shown anyone. Would you like your ears to be the first in the entire world to hear a song that's never been played to anyone or heard by anyone else?'

'Yes! I'd sure love that, Beryl.'

She lent down to her side bag attached to her chair and grabbed the sheet music and passed it to Timmo.

He looked at the title and read it to himself: *March for the Wounded*.

'I wrote this, thinking back to after the snake bit me on the legs.' Beryl sat at the piano and played a static bassline in the key of G, with her left hand to set the tempo. 'It's kind of a twelve-bar blues format with some of my own chordal ideas. Imagine the drums are like a slow military marching band.'

Beryl finished playing the song for Timmo, and after the last note faded out, she quietly said, 'You may think it's ironic, me writing that and not being able to march and all, but not matter what happens in life, we still need to move forward.'

Timmo was overjoyed to have heard it. 'Great tune, Beryl. The hits in bar ten are a stylish touch.' He was then stuck in contemplation. 'I think I'll try the guitar, like you say, ya know, and thanks for the Django Reinhardt record. I'll see you next week.'

March for the Wounded

Chapter Seventeen

THE CULTURALLY ENLIGHTENED

June 1981

Although Fred didn't have a black fella's vein in either arm or leg, he always felt deeply connected to the bush in the same way he had heard the local Aborigines speak about it, especially Bull and his mob.

Throughout the month of May, Fred had been watching re-runs of the 1976 documentary by Malcolm Douglas: *The Last of the Tribe.* Inspired by Malcolm's dedication to the Aboriginals, Fred decided to become more culturally informed and encompass respectful business practices regarding Aboriginal heritage surrounding the local areas.

He had been researching the traditions of the 'smoking ceremony', to welcome people into the town and give them a memorable experience. This learning was timed perfectly when Fred received his latest business asset in the post: the phone message service machine, which came from America.

During the last week, through talks with Bull and other locals, he learnt the name of the land and tribe wherein they lived, and for three days straight, he had been trying to change the phone welcome message to: 'Welcome to A Fine Motel, here in the heart of Duungidjawu Country, home of the Yuggera people. Please leave your name and number at the tone, and we will get back to you as soon as possible.' He spent hours trying to perfect it, but he felt that he wasn't using the correct pronunciation, which made him more frustrated.

He also reckoned a smoking ceremony to welcome new guests would not only be something that would help educate the tourists, but it could be a side bonus, bringing some added attention, possibly even newsworthy favours, resulting in dividends for the town and A Fine Motel.

He headed down to the pub over the weekend to have a catchup chat with Bull, to get his opinion and advice on these new ideas that may add value to the town.

Bull was originally named Bill. His name turned to Bull as a child when he was with his father at the cattle yards on his Uncle Jack's property over by Scrubby Creek Station, helping them run the cattle through the dip, and branding the new steers and heifers. They had all the cattle in one yard and were taking them up the run to jump into the water dip, when one of the wild bulls, known only as Grumpy, nudged it open and ran out across the yards, heading straight towards young Bill.

Grumpy's horns had grown unevenly, with the right one curving up in the normal way and the left one drooping down to the ground, which he used for scratching his ribs. It was unusual for a Brahman bull to have this feature, and little Bill believed that was what made the bull so grumpy.

Uncle Jack and Bill's father were too far away to reach him in time before Grumpy got loose and charged straight for Bill, kicking dust up as he sped. All Bill could think of doing was to stand his ground. He dug his bare feet into the earth, lent forward and opened out his arms while keeping his eyes locked with Grumpy, who was gaining momentum as he got closer to the boy. It looked as if little Bill was going to take on the bull and tackle the legs out from under it.

The bull raged, huffing and snorting towards Bill, and at the last minute, Bill dove out of the way like a miniature matador, just as his father rushed to pick him up, carrying him under one arm then running to the fence and climbing it like a rodeo clown as Grumpy circled around to return for another run up.

From then on, Bill was known as *Boorie* (little boy) Bull, until he became a teenager and just became Bull.

The jukebox already had a song playing when Fred

arrived at the bar. 'Girls on the Avenue' by Richard Clapton was into the first chorus. Fred loved that song, but it reminded him of a time he was on a convey to Rockhampton to work in Shoalwater Bay. It was playing on the radio in 1975, when he was heading out bush, and the heat was a killer in November. He had been unable to enjoy what he imagined others his age would be out doing with their life. It also reminded him of the ladies of the night he'd seen while walking the streets on his day of leave in Vietnam.

He grabbed two beers from Reg, and then he sat down with Bull at the table in the corner. On his walk from the bar to his table, he noticed the prospector named Cruickshank sitting in the opposite corner of the room with a map spread out on the table, making notes on grid paper. He made a mental note to try and ask this bloke more questions about what he was doing in town.

When Fred got to Bull's table, he began to tell him of his plans to use his newfound Aboriginal knowledge of language and the smoking ceremony 'welcome to country' traditions, with ideas to implement it for the motel guests when they arrived. Fred was excited and hoping to get some credit for his latest studies, and he looked to Bull for approval for what it may do for the town.

Bull was a big man with many small scars over his hands and knuckles, which came from cutting regrowth trees as a child on his Uncles Jack's land with a tomahawk, to keep the land clear so the grass could grow thick to fatten the cattle. Now that he was a boiler maker, he had spot burns on his forearms from sparks and slag of the welder.

Fred told him about his difficulties and how he attempted to record a phone message with the new message service machine, and he asked Bull if he would like to maybe record it for him. Although they were friends from school, Fred was slightly intimidated by the staunch stature of the guy.

Bull stared at Fred, making Fred question the entire last five minutes of his life, and just as a droplet of sweat pooled on Fred's left eyebrow, Bull said, 'Sounds a liddle racist to me, Fred.' And then he posed the question, 'Are you doing it to pay respect or to get some attention? You're not trying to cash in on my heritage, are you, white fella?'

Fred gulped then wiped the sweat that ran down his left cheek. He stood up, saying, 'Ah, nah … mate. Shit, Bull, I just realised I left the kettle on the boil … I gotta go, Bull, talk later.'

The publican, Reg, had been standing behind the bar listening in the entire time and chimed in, 'Good one, Bull, you've got him shitting bricks now!'

Bull gave him a grin and chuckled as he sipped his beer. 'Reckon I should tell him that anyone can do a "welcome to country"?'

'Nahh, let him sit on it a while!' Reg said with a deep belly laugh.

Bull then stood up from his chair and walked towards the men's toilets, passing where Cruickshank was sitting, and like a thunderous crack, he came down on Cruickshank, saying, 'You better not be up to something fishy, mate. Anyone tryin' to spoil our town will be hung out to dry like the lowdown dirty-rat-dog they are, aye!'

Reg chimed in from behind the bar, 'Bull, leave the man alone, he's just having a quiet beer.' He then turned to Cruickshank. 'You want to look at the menu, mate? It's on the house.'

Cruickshank stood up and replied in his thick nasal tone, 'No, I'll be leaving now anyway, as my work is done.' He stood up and folded away his map, placing it under his arm and neglecting to drink the remainder half-full schooner of beer sitting at the table. Then he walked out the door.

A few minutes passed, and Bull re-entered the main area to find Cruickshank gone.

Reg asked, 'Bull, what's a dirty-rat-dog?'

'Dunno, Reg, but I reckon sumthin' like the brother, Fredo Corleone, from *The Godfather*. Have you seen that movie?'

Chapter Eighteen

THE FREE PIE DAY!

June 1981

Week	Pie	Eggs	Total	For the Jar
1	$ 0.80	$ 1.10	$ 1.90	$ 0.10
2	$ 0.80	$ 1.10	$ 1.90	$ 0.10
3	$ 0.80	$ 1.10	$ 1.90	$ 0.10
4	$ 0.80	$ 1.10	$ 1.90	$ 0.10
5	$ 0.80	$ 1.10	$ 1.90	$ 0.10
6	$ 0.80	$ 1.10	$ 1.90	$ 0.10
7	$ 0.80	$ 1.10	$ 1.90	$ 0.10
8	$ 0.80	$ 1.10	$ 1.90	$ 0.10
9	$ 0.80	$ 1.10	$ 1.90	$ 0.10
10	$ 0.80	$ 1.10	$ 1.90	$ 0.10
11	$ 0.80	$ 1.10	$ 1.90	$ 0.10
12	$ 0.80	$ 1.10	$ 1.90	$ 0.10
13	$ 0.80	$ 1.10	$ 1.90	$ 0.10
14	$ 0.80	$ 1.10	$ 1.90	$ 0.10
15	$ 0.80	$ 1.10	$ 1.90	$ 0.10
16	$ 0.80	$ 1.10	$ 1.90	$ 0.10
17	$ 0.80	$ 1.10	$ 1.90	$ 0.10
18	$ 0.80	$ 1.10	$ 1.90	$ 0.10
19	$ 0.80	$ 1.10	$ 1.90	$ 0.10
20	Free Pie Day !!!			$ 1.90

Usually during Fred and Johno's pie-eating Monday routine, they'd find a different place to eat their pies. And while there weren't too many places in town to choose from, they had four or five places they'd usually go.

1. In front of the bakery, when they felt lazy.
2. Down by Dead Man's Creek waterhole, behind the town dump.
3. The undercover footy sheds on the town sports ground.
4. The park bench near the rusted tractor playground.

5. And occasionally, they would walk down the main street to see if Bull was at work in his welding shed.

Fred was always cautious about the tracks they walked, after the first and only time he accidentally kicked a loose street brick on his way out of Arthur's Bakery, causing the eggs he'd just bought to be thrown into the air, landing on the ground, splattering bright-yellow yolk and egg white all over the pavement.

When that happened, Margaret's chooks raced out and quickly ate the remains from the ground.

Johno was quick to point out, 'That's a bit bloody sick, ain't it, Fred?'

'In all their cuteness, chickens are ruthless creatures, mate,' Fred replied.

On this particular day, Fred waltzed back into the bakery to grab another carton of eggs, asking if he could come back later to drop off the money.

Margaret replied swiftly, 'Fred, don't worry about it. You take another carton and fix us up a drink next time we're at the pub.'

'Cheers, Marg! See you later, then,' Fred said as he walked out, holding his eggs firmly under his arm.

It was nearing winter solstice, so the sun was still sleeping on that crisp morning. Fred and Johno walked to the undercover footy sheds down by the sports oval to get protection against the chill of the wind and eat their pies. Here they began reminiscing about old times in high school and when they played rugby league together.

Fred recalled the trips they used to make in Johno's dad's Ford Fairlane to the next town over on Tuesdays and Thursdays for football training, and how they would share a six-pack of beer, throwing the empties at those religious street signs as they travelled along the highway heading back into town. 'Young and silly,' Fred decided they were back in those days.

After nineteen weeks, Fred was finally able to cash in on his savings and use up his self-awarded 'free pie voucher'. Often, Fred liked to keep his quirks private, not wanting them exposed to the townsfolk or even his friends.

Gathering up all his ten cent pieces into an envelope-sized terry towel zipper bag, he walked across town with Jessie in tow towards the bank, exchanging the ten cent coins for a two dollar note so that Johno and Arthur failed to detect any past transactional history that would raise suspicion as to Fred being frugal or weird with money.

He then walked out of the bank and met Johno in front of the massage parlour across the road from A Fine Motel, following their usual route down to the bakery. Johno had a story to tell Fred about Friday afternoon.

He told Fred how he had been travelling to the

neighbouring town to get chemical supplies for his septic truck when he was pulled over by the police for speeding. The officer approached his car and asked if he knew why he was being pulled over. Johno could detect a Scottish accent.

'Oh no, not the Toby jug?' Fred asked.

'Yeah, well, I may have been speeding a bit more than I should, but the memory of that "dirty Scott Corporal" on parade flashed back. So, you wanna know what I said to him? I said, "I can't hear you, I'm deaf!"'

The cop suspected Johno was trying to make light of the situation and swiftly punched Johno in the side of the head while he was sitting in the car.

Johno then jumped out from his car in a fit of frenzy and yelled, 'All you need is a punch in the face,' and he began to walk in a circular motion with his fists up. He got one good shot in before the nightstick was pulled out. And with a crack to the left knee, Johno went toppling over. 'I was in Nam, you bastard,' he yelled at the cop before he was cuffed and taken to jail.

The cop was new to the town and complacent with idiosyncrasies of the townsfolk, and he was totally unaware that Johno really was practically deaf in the right ear. However, after a few hours, the cop realised he was in the wrong and let Johno free without a fine for assault or speeding.

'Bloody Jesus, Johno, you're a wild operator! Glad you're all right. How's the knee?' Fred asked.

'Nothing a good pie can't make feel better.' Johno smiled and winked at Fred.

As they walked along Sale Street, Johno noticed how chipper Fred was today for a change, but he forgot to ask him why. When they arrived at the bakery and Fred told Jessie to sit and wait outside next to the wooden pole, she did as she was told, knowing full well the likelihood of tasty treats coming her way.

Margaret walked out saying good morning to them and placed a water bowl down by the pole for Jessie to drink. Jessie looked at Margaret as she walked away, as if to say, 'Is that it?'

Margaret started talking to Jessie and gave in. 'Okay, here you go, you big sook.' She pulled out a piece of pastry from her apron pocket and placed it on the red brick pavement in front of Jessie's snout.

Pleased with the outcome, Jessie wagged her tail in appreciation.

Johno entered the bakery, dividing the beaded curtain in two, and he moved quickly towards the heated pie shelf. He leant down to view the selection of pies through the glass window next to the counter. He took only a few seconds and selected his usual steak and mushy peas and paid Arthur at the counter. The peas in Arthur's pies were always glowing green, and Johno commended Arthur, yet again, for using the fresh local produce.

Fred had already picked up a dozen of Margaret's

free-range eggs and cradled them firmly like a baby between both forearms. He took a few more minutes to decide on what he wanted while Johno talked with Arthur about the football results over the weekend, and the highly anticipated second match of state representative teams to be selected after the success of the 1980 inaugural rugby league 'State of Origin' match. Fred decided on steak, cheese and bacon.

Arthur was shocked, then remarked, 'Fred, you never buy that one. What's going on? You get lucky last night, eh?'

Fred looked back at Arthur and coldly responded, 'If by "lucky" you mean I woke up alive today, then yeah.'

Johno had sat down on the silver chair in the corner to wait and commented how he'd noticed Fred had an extra spring in his step this morning, 'Strutting like he was Errol Flynn entering a neon bloody ballroom!'

Just as Fred was about to pay, Arthur asked, as per usual, if Fred wanted sauce with his pie.

Fred replied, also as per usual, 'No thanks, I'm watching my sugar intake.'

Arthur was quick to reply, 'Oh for fuck's sake, Fred.'

'ARTHUR!' Margaret belted out.

He turned towards Margaret. 'Sorry, love.' Then he looked at Fred. 'Fred, take it, it's on the house.'

Fred reached in the bowl and grabbed a tiny squeeze sauce from the glass bowl. 'Thanks, mate!

Johno and Fred turned and exited through the beaded curtain. They both called out,

'See ya, Arthur, bye Marg!'

Jessie jumped up, and the three of them walked down the dirt street to the CWA-sponsored park bench near the kid's rusty tractor playground and sat facing each other.

Johno kept on the footy game topic. He was extremely excited with the hope for a repeat of the 1980 win when Queensland beat those New South Welshman and how King Wally and Big Artie Beetson would destroy those 'dirty cockroach bastards', leading the Cane Toads to victory once again. Johno was the first to take a bite out of his pie.

Jessie stared at Fred, who talked to her like a young child, saying, 'Okay, girl, you can have one now,' referring to the eggs. And then he removed one from its carton and cracked it and dropped it on the concrete ground under the table for Jessie to lick up. Fred was more methodical with his approach to pie eating. He removed the pie from the brown paper bag, then placed the bag flat onto the wooden tabletop like a makeshift plate, with the pie sitting on top. Fred then held the tiny squeeze bottle of sauce and pointed it towards the pie. He took a deep breath in, then exhaled like a meditative practice, much like the way his father did before pulling the trigger of his rifle. He squeezed the tiny sauce bottle, which released a shot of bright-red tomato sauce flying in slow motion.

Fred and Johno both watched, but somehow Fred froze, unable to react in time. The sauce sailed through the air like a scarlet missile tracking on path, landing right on the crotch of Fred's tan pants. The look on Fred's face was both of anguish and disgust. He yelled out with a thick tone, 'GET FUCKED, ARTHUR!'

Johno instantly burst out laughing, unable to contain the pie in his mouth, sending brown and bright green exploding through the air, hitting Fred in the face.

As the green peas dripped down on his shirt, Fred erupted with three quick sneezes and, with no time to cover his mouth, sprayed Johno in the face with some of the same pie that came from his own mouth!

They both looked over to the park swing set and saw a mother setting up to push her child on the swing; she was looking straight at them with eyes only a disapproving mother could gleam.

Johno was quiet for a second or two before saying, 'You and your bloody sinusitis, Fred.'

Then they burst out in laughter again, until the blow-flies started buzzing around Fred's face.

Fred, lost for words, had his first doctor's appointment later that day with the psychologist in the city. He said to Johno, 'Bloody Arthur, how am I meant to go to my appointment looking like this?'

Johno reached into his pocket and passed him his

napkin. 'There's a tap over there, go clean yourself up. You'll be right, mate.'

Fred hated to admit that this time Johno was right.

Chapter Nineteen

THE FIRST SESSION

June 1981

Fred had now cleaned himself up from the mess that was his twenty-week-reward free pie day. He'd been thinking heavily ever since his conversation with Bull last Saturday. He felt strongly that he wasn't a racist, but he realised it would be something he would need to discuss with the psychologist, along with the spontaneous sneezing … or sinusitis … whatever it was.

He left earlier than planned, to give himself time to call into the nursery and check out some new garden ideas for the motel. He ended up getting a dozen coca palms.

After the palms were loaded into Fred's car, he managed to get to the city earlier than expected. He pulled into the doctor's office car park at the front of the main entrance and decided to get a warm coffee and bite to eat for lunch somewhere nearby. He found a café and went inside.

Paddington seemed dirty to him, compared to the bush. *A forgotten area, maybe,* he thought as he sat down at the veranda table overlooking Brisbane city. A currawong called out from the gums that almost hindered the view of the city. *A magpie's bastard brother or a crow's cautious cousin?*

He sat at the café looking over the suburbs surrounding the city, wondering how it all got to where it was today. Large red brick buildings had now popped up, and the house block sizes had reduced to a quarter acre and were squeezed into any remaining areas. He remembered the times as a child when the family visited Pearl's parents here and how spacious the land-to-house ratio was then. *It used to be acreage all over there.*

Fred looked at his watch and jumped up to get to his appointment. He walked down the concrete tile pathway along Given Terrace, then went into the office building, removing his hat as he walked through the door.

When he approached the reception desk, Fred was quick to notice the attractive woman sitting there reading. 'I'm here to see Doctor Liebrand. It's my first visit,' he told her.

The woman appeared surprised when she looked up from the magazine she had been reading, putting it in the desk draw and closing it abruptly. However, Fred was fast to catch a glimpse of the front cover: *Penthouse Forum.*

'Please have a … seat … Mr … uh, please just have a seat, Doctor *Leibbrandt* will be out soon.' She smiled at him cheekily.

Fred looked closely at her name badge: Holly. He then casually walked to the waiting area and looked once more over his shoulder to peak at her. He noticed how silky her dark-brown hair was that flowed along the curve of her face, the tips almost kissing each other under her chin. The colour of her eyes, shaped like almonds, matched her hair … and then he kicked his foot on the leg of the coffee table. Fred looked down at his foot, hoping nobody heard the dull squeaking noise it made before he carefully lifted the table to move it back to its place.

He sat in the waiting room, listening to the loud tick-tock of the white plastic clock in the corner, observing the collection of sprawled-out generic *Women's Day* and *Better Homes and Gardens* magazines on the coffee table. He was the only one in the room apart from Holly, who had already furtively started reading *Penthouse Forum* again.

Fred tried to guess her age and settled on twenty-nine. *She looks old enough to know her way around streets, but not old enough for any cracks in the pavement to show.* He felt the need to check himself, and his inner dialogue continued. *Not that cracks are bad – shows maturity, which can be quite attractive.*

Fred lent forward and flicked over the magazine

options laid out in front of him. *It'd be nice to be in an adult-only-style waiting room, as it would encourage people to arrive early.* Not pleased with the selection on offer, he stood up and took a few steps towards the reception desk to ask, 'Is there, umm … anything else more interesting that I could perhaps read?'

But at this moment, the main door opened, and an old man who was holding on tightly to a walking stick slowly motioned towards the reception.

So, Fred hastily turned and sat back down, waiting. He looked down at his sauce-stained suit pants with splotches on his shirt, then over at the old man's stained shirt. *Shit, I must look like a bloody idiot.* He had even decided to leave his jacket in the car because it had more marks left on it. *Bloody Arthur!*

Suddenly, the hallway door opened, revealing a woman wearing no shoes, ripped denim shorts with a short-sleeve army-green shirt half-tucked in. She walked towards the counter and paid for her session. Fred assumed she looked to be in a worse situation than he was. *I wonder what her problem is?* Then he remembered what his dad said about opinions being like arseholes, similarly: 'to assume is to make an ass out of you and me'.

The scraggly haired woman handed Holly a cheque at the counter.

Holly looked at the cheque and said, 'It's missing a signature.'

The woman snatched it back off Holly and held it up to examine it. 'I'll have to go see Dad and come back.'

As she walked out the door, the woman snarled at Fred silently, and Fred replied by giving a polite but anxious smile with raised eyebrows as she walked out. He sat quietly for a moment and heard Holly talking on the phone.

'Barry fell in the pool last night. I couldn't sleep and noticed he wasn't home yet, so I got up to get some water, then heard this noise outside. He literally came swaggering in, banging the door behind. He was saturated, and it was three am … I'm so tired today.'

She paused and glanced across the room at Fred before saying, 'Yes, he's ready.' She called out to Fred, 'The doctor will now see you.'

Fred stood up and slowly walked over. 'Barry likes a drink, hey?' he asked Holly.

Holly looked at him with a puzzled expression.

'Yes, I understand how it is. I just quit drinking a few months ago, well sort of … as I still have the occasional beer, but I've more or less given up.'

With a smirk, Holly stared at him and said, 'Barry's my cat. He fell in the pool last night.'

Fred, realising he may have given away some sensitive information about himself, replied with the first thing that came to his mind, 'Well, you know, I've always thought there was nothing like a wet pussy at three in the morning.'

Holly laughed, but before she could say anything in return, the hallway door opened to reveal a black woman wearing a navy-blue blazer and stylish glasses. She glanced at her notepad, and then without looking up, said in a sharp, assertive tone, 'Fred Fine.'

Fred realised it must be his doctor, and he quickly recalled the topics he needed to discuss with her. Then he gulped, trying to contain a sneeze, but it released short, fast and into his hat. He smiled at Holly as he walked past her desk, and she grinned and winked at him.

When Fred walked down a short hallway, he noticed the neatly carved pale-blue trim around the ceiling, and it reminded him of the pattens on the dress Holly was wearing.

Doctor Leibbrandt stood at the door to her office and said, 'Please go in and take a seat.'

Fred walked into the room and looked at the two seats, then back at the doctor.

'Either one is fine,' the doctor said.

He sat in the seat to the left, closest to the window, and thought, *it might make a quick escape if things start to get awkward.*

There was a moment of silence, which gave Fred time to drink in the room and notice foreign provocative artwork-style bookends; two books stuck out: *The Manual of Psychology* and a book by Freud. Then Fred realised the doctor was staring at his crotch and remembered the stains from earlier. So, without being prompted, he decided to explain, 'Yeah, well, I had an incident with a pie this morning and had no time to change.'

'It happens,' she sympathised.

'Well, it only happened cause of this sneeze I can't seem to shake,' Fred admitted.

'Okay, well, before we talk about that, I'll start our first session by sharing some things about me.'

Fred appreciated this moment to sit in silence and listen to the doctor share 'her story'. As he listened, he couldn't help but notice a scar behind her left ear that fell to the top of her neckline. He imagined her to be a strong woman; she had muscular legs built for running, and she looked like she 'meant business'. Her hair was perfectly placed in a ponytail, and Fred guessed her to be mid-thirties. She was still young enough to care how she presented herself, and there were no crow's feet; her taught skin matched her tightly worn short skirt that was paired with a double-breasted blazer, which led him to assume she was an incredibly determined person and not afraid to roll up her sleeves if need be. Her exposed shins were silky looking, and her skin almost shone in the fluorescent ceiling light, and when she looked at him, he noticed how piercing her eyes were. Fred couldn't help but think that they could see into his soul.

As a young girl, Doctor Lina Leibbrandt grew up on a 20,000-hectare game-hunting property in South Africa.

Her father had Dutch heritage and her mother African. They were unique in that few mixed-race couples existed in that part of the world, especially in that era. When she was only eight years old, a group of masked men broke into the secured homestead, killing both her parents, and they stole her as she slept. The scary man with the facial scarring told her that her parents' land was their land and that they were going to hold her until her uncle paid them the money they deserved.

'That's part one of my personal introduction to trauma, and if you want to know more, I'll tell you part two during our next session. Now, let's talk about your challenges. When did this first sneeze occur?'

Fred took a moment to consider, 'Ahh … it was just after I got the letter from my sister telling me that our mother was in hospital and to come home.'

'And where were you?'

'Townsville.'

'What were you doing in Townsville?'

'I was in the army.'

'Okay, I think we're going to start again; I only have an hour with you, so let's get to the crucks of it. What caused the first sneezing outburst?'

'As I said, I got a letter saying to come home, but my rat CO, ginger nuts Peto, denied my leave application.'

'Sorry, what year and when was this?'

'I was in Townsville, end of 77.'

'Go on.' The doctor smiled encouragingly at him.

'Ah, yeah, anyway … so I took things into my own hands … I had no other option.'

'Right. So, how did this all transpire?'

Fred described the past events as best as he could. Mostly, he felt he was babbling and not making sense, jumping from the Vietnam war to jail, then trying to tie it to the present.

The time past slowly as Fred watched the clock in the corner. He was unable to pin down or understand why the doctor was asking if and how often he had stomach issues and if he ever experienced reflux pains.

The doctor finally asked Fred, 'Are you well-read, Fred?'

Confused, Fred thought, *Red?* 'I ain't no communist!'

She replied, 'No, I meant: do you read often?'

Fred shook his head. 'No, I've got more fingers on one hand than I've read books.'

The doctor replied, 'Have you heard of *The Catcher in the Rye*?' She took a few steps to the bookshelf behind her.

Fred noticed her left stocking had a ladder up the side and looked away.

She then turned and said, 'Okay, here's some home-work before your next session. See how far you can get through this book and start putting your thoughts onto paper. I want you to write down how you feel when this "sneeze" happens or when you feel strange. And keep track of your stomach and gastro-reflux issues.' She paused for a moment before going on, 'It wouldn't be so bad to put yourself in the spotlight, look at the man in the mirror and make a change, and be prepared for some harder conversations next time we meet, okay?'

Fred wasn't sure about his 'homework', but he was willing to give it a try. 'Sure, Doc, thanks for that.' He then walked back out to the reception area.

When Holly passed him the invoice, she asked, 'Where have you travelled from today?'

Fred paused, then replied, 'I came in from Duungidjawu Country. It's about three or four hours from here. I'm heading back today, but the next time I have an appointment, I'll probably stay overnight.'

Holly looked at him and remarked, 'Oh, really, you'll enjoy that.'

Fred was quick to reply, 'Yeah, I've never stayed in a penthouse before, might hav'ta get one of those.'

Holly blushed, and then her rich-brown eyes beheld Fred's blue eyes as she replied with a warm tone, 'Well, we look forward to your next visit, Mr Fine.'

He softly smiled. 'I'm looking forward to it now … uh not that I have anything wrong with me, just a darn sneeze that won't go, you see … Okay, yep, see you then.' He turned and walked out the door and put his hat on, not noticing his brown leather wallet fall from his pocket and land on the floor inside the reception room.

Holly, however, spotted its fall and waited for Fred to return. When she heard Fred's car engine start, she rolled her eyes before quickly shuffling over in her heels to pick it up, and then she raced out of the office to try and catch Fred. She tapped on his car window. 'You might need this!'

'Ah … yeah, thanks a lot,' Fred replied, following with, 'next time I'm in the city, lunch is on me, okay?'

Holly took a second to respond, but she agreed, nodding her head and saying, 'Maybe … if you play your cards right.'

Fred had already put the car in reverse, and he slowly exited the car park, unable to take his eyes off her. He even tipped his hat as he drove out of the car park, and she gave a nervous wave.

When he drove off, his mind was racing with surprise and disbelief of how well he just interacted with Holly. It had been a long time since he tried flirting with someone, so long he couldn't remember.

As he travelled home reflecting on the session with the doctor and the things she advised, Fred popped an old tape into the stereo; he hadn't heard the band for a while. It was a New Zealand band called Dragon. His favourite song on that tape was 'April Sun in Cuba', and when that snare hit, Fred would scrunch his mouth and nose up as if he was deep in the pocket alongside the drummer.

He liked the doctor's suggestion of starting a journal

and trying to describe what his anxiety felt like, especially after he sneezed. He'd not put pen to paper since Vietnam and Townsville days; he had almost forgotten how much he enjoyed writing. It would help him become more grounded with the world he now lived in and his new life post-military. He also thought about Holly and wondered what she liked to do for fun. He knew he was quite smitten, but realising it was unlikely anything would happen between them, he quickly moved on to focusing on his driving and the things he needed to do when he arrived home. *Might start painting the fence tomorrow.*

Fred then tried to remember where he put his collection of poems and journals back at the motel. As the chorus to the song kicked in, Fred started to sing, and he decided that it wasn't such a bad idea to get a hotel next time, to enjoy the city and time away from work.

The glowing sunset was crimson with smooth transitions to magenta that afternoon, and when he arrived home, he remarked, 'God's country.'

It was just on dark when he pulled the cord light in the storage shed to start searching for where his flight case and bag were, where all his army items were kept safe. He found his old bayonet, and sitting just on top of the box were the letters from his mum and the writing he worked on while overseas.

He picked up the poem on top. It was titled:

Treble and Bass. His mother had written it and sent it to him not long after he joined the army. Fred read aloud.

'Treble and bass, my saving grace
Somewhere in the middle, surrounded by space
Explode like a star and burn as I land
Into a black hole, which shrinks and expands

Sometimes things are forte sometimes decrescendo
How I am so grateful for this upright piano
It only plays minor, diminished by grief
The turn of events to me beggars' belief.
A pit of love a pit of hate
An interesting slurry, the happens of late
Surely all scars heal and come to mend?
Not knowing how long I look for the bend.

Seeping in seeping out, an augmented self
The speakers, my friends, and my wealth
My only care, a pair saving grace,
My only two loves, are Treble and Bass.'

Pearl had later told him that although it was inspired by music, it was written not long after Frank's death. Treble and bass were tributes, or references, to Beryl and himself.

He flicked through a few more pages and found the

poem called *If,* which his mother copied from one of her books by handwriting the poet Rudy Kipling's work. She explained that it was first published in 1910.

If you can keep your head when all about you
Are losing theirs and blaming it on you,
If you can trust yourself when all men doubt you,
But make allowance for their doubting too;
If you can wait and not be tired by waiting,
Or being lied about, don't deal in lies,
Or being hated, don't give way to hating,
And yet don't look too good, nor talk too wise:

If you can dream—and not make dreams your master;
If you can think—and not make thoughts your aim;
If you can meet with Triumph and Disaster
And treat those two impostors just the same ...

He continued to read on, with every line forming a connection to his life at present and believing his mother sent it to him ten years earlier to help his young mind work over the good and troubled times he was going through.

Hearing a vehicle arrive back at one of the rooms, he walked to the front to see which car it was. Fred still held the letter in his hand. 'Cruickshank!' He squeezed and his hand tightly crumpled the handwritten poem.

He then looked at his hand and yelled, 'Shit!' He quickly tried to flatten the paper on tabletop while looking out the window. *I wonder what he's been up to lately.* The white Land Cruiser looked clean, unlike any poor prospecting fool's truck that chased dreams in the hills for gold. *I'll suss him out further first thing tomorrow morning!*

Chapter Twenty

THE CHINESE TAKEAWAY

July 1981

Fred was in the kitchen boiling eggs. He treated himself to one takeaway meal per month, which he enjoyed while watching *60 Minutes*. The meal he was savouring tonight was from Ming's Very Good Chinese Takeaway. Ming's had only been open for eight years but was already a rundown restaurant with cracked bricks running along the façade. It had pink-framed French doors and bright-chartreuse borders around the shop walls, and curtains were strung with up wire. Fred would pay for Beryl, as a treat for them both.

As usual, Beryl commented on the peas in the special fried rice, exclaiming, 'I don't know why they feel the need to put *peas* in there. Ask them not to put any peas in the fried rice, please! It doesn't add anything to the rice.'

Fred didn't mind them, but he recalled a disturbing

dream after their Chinese meal last month, which was about an accidentally baited koala stuck in the fence screaming. In the dream, Fred was standing over the koala with a .22-calibre rifle, trying to work up the courage to put it out of its misery when he heard a high-pitched ringing and then heard the song 'Mellow Yellow', by Donovan, fade into the dream. He paused, not wanting to pull the trigger, but he did so.

He told Beryl, 'I woke up in a pool of sweat to the radio alarm blasting "Mellow Yellow". I hope that dream doesn't happen again,' he said as he served up their customary Chinese order.

Apart from a squeak of Beryl's wheels as she shifted her place in the room, there was an awkward ten seconds of silence between them.

That night, one of the segments on *60 Minutes* was an interview with the maniac murderer Charles Manson. Fred noticed he became twitchy while listening to it. Some of the things Manson said resonated with Fred, which worried him.

When Ray Martin came onto the screen, Beryl commented, 'Oh that Ray's got spunk. He's such a dreamboat, those eyes, and that sexy, sexy voice.'

Ray's segment was mainly speculative on the up-and-coming royal wedding of Prince Charles and Diana, and the location of their honeymoon, spruiking, 'Rumour has it that the prince and soon-to-be princess will be making the trip "down under" to experience the outback and submersing themselves in Aboriginal culture.'

Fred remarked, 'Perfect, see? Another bonus of us getting in touch with our Aboriginal brothers.'

Beryl stared at him judgmentally.

Fred added one last thing. 'And sis*ters*?' he said with trepidation.

'What did your psychologist say about your conversation with Bull earlier this week?' Beryl asked with cheeky undertones.

Fred ignored her.

'Always with the bloody peas in the fried rice, Fred!' Beryl remarked as she picked them out one by one with her fork and shuffled them into a pile on the plastic lid container on the coffee table.

They opened the bag of fortune cookies, and each read their note.

Beryl recited, 'You have a secret admirer ... Pfft!' she scoffed. 'Like hell I do.'

Fred looked at his message and read it out, 'Follow your dreams, and fortune will follow.' He paused. 'I hope I don't follow my last dream about the koala,' he remarked.

With the ticking of the clock on the television program signalling the end of the show, Fred told Beryl he was off to bed for an early night, as there were guests arriving tomorrow and he wanted to be well rested for when they arrived.

He walked into his bedroom, got changed into his flannelette pyjamas, then turned the lights off and laid his head down on the pillow, closing his eyes. He was almost asleep until he remembered he had forgotten to do the laundry, and then he sneezed!

Half-asleep and still thinking about the Manson interview, he begrudgingly got out of bed and mumbled under his breath while walking to the laundry. 'Dying is easy, aye, Manson … is it, though …' He pondered this vaguely for a moment. 'Yeah, it's definitely the easy way out,' he agreed with Manson.

He put a load of washing on and went back into his room and laid down in bed. After laying there for what seemed like at least twenty minutes, he tried to get to sleep, but his mind kept wandering.

After twenty minutes, he was becoming more frustrated with every minute that passed. So, he decided to get up and write something down to help shift his mind onto something else. He picked up a pen and found some blank index sheet paper in the second draw down and wrote:

Rain on me
Put me down pin me back,
Put me up against the wall don't let me in
chew on me with your teeth, suffocate me underneath
Just like bullets, the rain feels falling now

*Too late to start over again, final phase is spinning me
round
Round and round inside my head as the whirlpool drags
me down.*

Fred put his pen down and read what he had just penned. Reflecting on it all, he said to himself, 'Shit, I need to start writing some positive stuff … this just feels even more depressing.' The cool air gave Fred a sharp shiver up his spine, and he walked out to see if Jessie wanted to come inside for the night. 'It's a bit cold tonight, isn't it, girl.'

Jessie looked up at Fred as he stood at the door on the veranda, her tail slowly wagging with anticipation.

'Come in then … hop into your bed down there.' He pointed at a sheepskin rug on the floor. 'And don't think about jumping into my bed tonight like last time.' He turned off the lamp and laid his head back down on the pillow.

Drifting off to sleep, he murmured some phrases the Manson had said in the interview on the television that night: *'Where would I go?'* and *'Gotta catch on, boy, road's rough.'*

As Fred finally managed to drift off to sleep on that icy winter night, he was quick to begin lucid dreaming of being in love with a beautiful brunette girl with almond-shaped eyes and pouty lips. Fred quickly realised she resembled Holly from the doctor's reception desk that week. They were bushwalking along a thin walking trail with thick green vegetation and bright-yellow button daisies peppered between large boulders alongside the track.

With Jessie following, who fell far back behind them, Fred and Holly both stopped to wait for Jessie to catch up. Fred could see the faceless man from previous dreams slowly spinning, sitting on a flat rock under a tree further along the track, and he chose to ignore it. Once Jessie caught up, she decided to have a quick poo behind a nearby tree.

They all then took a few more steps and arrived at an opening to a picnic spot with magnificent views across the valley, highlighting the curvature of the dense bushland and gullies that feed into the creeks below. They stopped, and then Fred prepared the pre-packed romantic brunch from the basket he was carrying.

He laid out the red- and black-checked blanket and placed the basket in the middle. They sat on the edge of the blanket, with Jessie behind them. The breeze was gently caressing their faces as they enjoyed cheese and crackers.

Suddenly, the wind changed direction, and slowly, Fred started to smell something not so pleasant. He sniffed the cheese to confirm it was still fresh, and it wasn't the cheese. And then he finally realised that the smell was of Jessie's earlier bowel movements, and it was getting stronger by the minute.

Fred wasn't sure if Holly could smell anything, and he was too shy to ask, for fear of ruining whatever atmosphere they had. He looked out over the view and decided to comment on how lovely the colours of the valley were, when the landscape abruptly changed into an open-cut mine with large walls carved into the side of the mountains. Earthmoving equipment was positioned on several aspects of spoiled land, and mammoth dump trucks travelled slowly up and down the track to a crushing plant that was tipping a brownish, blackish ore into a big funnel. Cars resembling the 'new to town' big company vehicles looked more like matchbox cars driving around the extra wide roads.

Fred's heart began to beat faster as the sky got darker, and it became harder to breath. Fred noticed Holly started to sniff by scrunching up her nose, and he tried to ignore what he also smelt.

They sat on the rug, continuing to eat the cheese and crackers when Fred heard a stick snap in the woods nearby, and he tried to spot whatever was out there. When he looked back into Holly's eyes, he sensed that someone must be watching them. He then started to sweat with the notion of being spied on and experienced flashbacks to being in the army, scouting his section through the jungle in Vietnam.

Then Fred changed places with another body in the same bushland, and he was running through the leaves and low-lying branches that were brushing past his face, but at the same time, he was almost gliding through the woods, silently pushing everything aside with no obstructions.

He stared at his arms and legs, which were completely covered in thick brown matted, bear-like fur. He couldn't understand why he was running, or why he was covered in fur.

'What is going on?' he asked as he ran. 'And how am I able to run so heavily without making a sound?' He stopped abruptly when he stood on a stick, making a loud crack. At that moment, he peered through the bushes and saw himself and Holly sitting on the rug eating, with Jessie sitting behind. The outlook of what was a beautifully treed valley had turned into a scared and unsightly open-cut mine. He smelt the dog poo even stronger now. At that moment, he realised he had somehow transformed into a yowie. He looked down at the bottom of his hairy yowie foot and then gagged and almost vomited when he realised he stepped in dog poo.

Holly looked deep into the other Fred's eyes, pursed her lips and asked, 'Do you smell dog shit?'

Fred woke suddenly in a pool of sweat to see Jessie taking a massive dump right in front of his face on his bed, and Fred projectile vomited, covering the clothes he had put out over the dressing table ready for the day ahead. He then pulled the bedsheets off, put them in the laundry and cleaned himself up.

'What the hell was that all about, Jess? You've never done that before … that's the last time you sleep inside, sorry to say it, girl.'

Jessie looked down at the ground with shame, as if to say, 'Sorry, Fred.'

He then sat at the dining table and ate some breakfast. Beryl had made coffee, for a change; Fred was usually particular about his coffee. The dream was still heavy on his mind; it was devastating to think of a mine in his back-yard and the land being absolutely ruined for corporate greed. He started to think about the vehicle Cruickshank drove and for once and for all, getting to the bottom of what he was doing in town.

He sipped his coffee then called out to Beryl. 'Gee, Beryl, what did you do to this coffee? And did you give the dog something weird to eat last night?'

She called, 'Aye, what's wrong with it? And as for Jessie, no … I don't think so?'

Fred took another sip and called back, 'It tastes like it's been strained through a shit farmer's sock; I don't know what you've done, but I'll make another in a second.'

Chapter Twenty-One
THE PASSING OF PEARL FINE

August 1977

The sun was yet to rise as the men stood stretching their legs at the bottom of Castle Hill. It was a steady incline, and by midway, their glutes and quads started to burn. The troop did this trek each week, and they enjoyed it, or pretended to if they didn't; they may have only enjoyed the rivalry and team environment. The ocean view from the top, looking over to Magnetic Island with sun light sparkling across the water, was satisfying, compared to their usual work environment.

Laverack Barracks was purpose-built and placed strategically in Far North Queensland during conflict in Southeast Asia and the Cold War tensions. The troop made it to the top of the hill climb and were given a five-minute rest before descending. Once completed, they jumped on the back of the uni-mog vehicle and were transported back to base.

Once Fred was showered then changed into army greens, he sauntered over to headquarters to collect the mail. He felt fresh and clean, a rarity for an infantry soldier who spent more than half the year out bush or in the jungle. The air still had a crispness about it, though winter in Townsville wasn't as cold as in Australia's southern states; it was a tropical climate and either hot or warm all year round. He collected the troops' letters from the administrator's desk at headquarters. It was mid-month, and he was surprised to see a letter for himself.

Pearl's letters usually arrived at the beginning of each month. This one was from home but had different hand-writing to his mothers. He removed the rubber band and placed the remaining stack of letters in the centre of the table for the other troops to collect in their own time, and then he headed into his office. Fred opened his letter and quickly made out that Beryl had written it this time; she never had written till now, and her past messages were from within Pearl's letters.

Hi Fred,
I tried calling your unit, but the number rings out.
Mum is not well, and the doctor said she hasn't got long.
They've taken her to the RBH hospital.
Come home, please.

Without hesitation, Fred pulled a 'leave application form' from the desk draw and applied for two weeks off. Then he delivered it to the newly appointed commanding officer; he'd never taken too much leave during his service, so completing this form himself, instead of approving one for another was new to him.

Captain Peterson, a tall, gangly man with fire engine-red hair and a monotone-nasally voice, was still on his own physical training run around the base. 'Peto' was a strong long-distance runner and often chose to train on flat ground by himself instead of with the troop most mornings. All the boys quietly knew this was the opposite of what a well-respected leader would be known for. The previous lieutenant had been posted out one month earlier, so Fred reported directly to Captain Peterson until the new one arrived.

The clerk in the office assured Fred, 'I'll hold onto this and pass it to Captain Peterson as soon as he arrives.'

'Thanks, Corporal Ember, and make sure he knows to speak to me to discuss everything before he completes his end,' asked Fred.

On returning to his own office, he made a call to home, which rung out.

The boys in the troop were all showered and in uniform, mucking around with each other in the room next door.

'Oye, Jimbo, what'd you do last night?'

'Saw you chundered halfway up the hill.'

'Me and Woodsy were out till four this morning on Flinders Street trying to pick-up, barely got two hours sleep … feeling a bit green today.'

'I'm getting too old for this shit,' mumbled Fred as he stood up to address the troop. 'Guys, take the vehicles to the wash bay, and after they're clean, check the fluids and tyre pressure.'

The boys went to the grab the keys and left the donga. This gave Fred some peace and quiet. And so, he waited for a response or call from Captain Peto to discuss his leave application. But after three hours, there was still nothing. His internal response was, *he's ignoring me, what a weak bastard.*

Just before lunch, he checked in with Ember again for an update, but Ember hadn't heard anything back from Peto.

By now, the boys had brought back clean troopies; Fred grabbed the keys for one and jumped in. He took off around the base, looking for Peto while trying to maintain composure, for the conversation couldn't go his way without it. As he drove past the officer's mess, Fred noticed the flaming red-haired weasel through the closed glass window.

He wasn't allowed to enter the officer's mess, so he stopped short and waited for Peto to leave the building. Trying to simmer his mind, and not think the worst about his mother, he began to form the right words in his head.

It was obvious Peto was dodging confrontation.

Then without warning, Fred sneezed explosively into his right elbow. He was then hit with dizziness and a blurry-clouded vision. He sat still and re-gripped the steering wheel firmly as his heart rate started to increase with a heavy thump like it was attempting to jump out from his chest. His clouded vision turned coloured with patches of reds and violet. His breath increased and became rapid. *Is this what it's like to be blind? How long will this last?*

He heard the crows call to each other behind the building as they flew into the bins to squabble over discarded food the cooks threw out with the completion of the lunch service. Fred was still blinded and sat frozen in the troop carrier, unable to move. *Is this what Beryl felt when she woke up without her legs? Will I ever be able to see again?*

After some time – he wasn't sure how long had passed – his breath started to regulate once again, and the colourful patches that blinded his eyes slowly subsided like rain clouds clearing after a storm. Looking into the officer's mess, he could see it had cleared out. 'Goddamn it!' he yelled.

Feeling well enough to drive, Fred went back to headquarters and into the administration office to find Peto, but he had gone out again to a base commander meeting.

Ember did explain though that he left Fred's application form there. Ember passed it to Fred.

There in big red letters was stamped: *Denied*.

Fred stomped back to his office.

The rest of the troop had returned from lunch and waited for Fred's orders to take them through the remainder of the afternoon. So, on the way past them, he told the boys, 'You lot have the next three hours to get any admin done before the live fire field exercise next week.'

The next morning, Fred finally cornered Peto in his office and asked for an explanation.

The nasal response was not in Fred's favour.

'Sergeant, as you know, we have the live fire exercise starting next week, and without a lieutenant to lead the troop, you are far too important to the regiment. We need you here.'

It was in that moment that Fred felt the need to unburden himself with the weight of his conditions, which were causing distaste in his mind about the army he once loved. 'Sir, this place has been hard to live with for a long time, over ten years now, and I can't go on anymore.'

Peto stared back and responded, 'I guess that's not a decision for me, and you have a choice to make then.'

Fred knew he had no other option, and time was not on his side.

That afternoon, he packed everything he could grab, putting it into an army-issue canvas bag and flight trunk. He wasn't packing for the live fire exercise; he was packing for home. He figured – *if that rat Peto is going to be a bastard about this then* – he would have no other option but to take off and go AWOL, rather than beg and plead his case.

When he was done, he looked around the room and his eyes struck the bayonet in the cupboard. He said *why not* to himself and threw it on top of the bag and zipped it up.

He then dialled a taxi, which took him to the local truck depot at Thuringowa Central.

Once there, he placed his belongings by a water post and walked from truck to truck, trying to find the next truck heading south for Brisbane. Knocking on each truck door waiting to hear a response from a resting driver, he finally found a fellow named Terry, who had just woken.

Terry said that he would be leaving soon and could drop him off.

As Fred walked over to grab his gear, he knew the next twenty-four to forty-eight hours were surely going to test his patients. He had still not been able to contact

Beryl; he had a feeling she would be with their mother at the Royal Brisbane Hospital and figured he would go straight there.

Terry's truck rattled in places as it sat idling, but when it got into gear, those noises petered out and the engine growled and revved loudly through the gears until they got above eighty kilometres, and then it started to quieten down, enough for Terry to ask, 'So, Fred, what type of music do you like?'

The question hadn't been asked of Fred since high school. 'Not sure, really … I like all sorts, I guess.'

'Well, let me tell you, I was driving up from Melbourne a few months ago and had a stopover in Sydney. I ended up at the Pav, ya know the Pav?'

'Nah, not really, mate,' Fred admitted.

Terry continued, 'The Hordern Pavilion, it's in Moores Park, not far from the city. Anyway, I caught Sherbet play at the Pav last month, and while I was there … have you heard of Sherbet?'

'What do they sing?' asked Fred.

'Come on … "Howzat" was number one on the charts last year.'

'Oh yep, I know that one.'

Terry paused before saying in a nervous tone, 'Umm, hey your … ah … what do I care, you're stuck here now, aren't-cha.' He laughed. 'So, I was doing some LSD with these others at the show, and they gave me a bootleg copy, an unreleased Richard Clapton tape. Wanna hear it? They have this amazing track, well I think it's amazing, called 'Deep Water'. I don't know any other Aussie band quite like these guys.' Terry reached for the tape in the centre of the dash and placed it in the cassette player.

'Terry, have you got any acid on you now?'

With the essence of craze in his eyes, Terry looked over at Fred and confirmed, 'I might have had a pinch already today before we left the truck stop.'

'Really?'

'Yeah, mate, it's called a microdose ... helps me stay alert and awake. All I need to do is stay in my lane, and everything will be a-okay.'

His reassurance wasn't felt by Fred.

Fred listened to the Richard Clapton song 'Deep Water' blaring, knowing he himself was in deep shit in more ways than one. The voice inside his head said, *strap in, Fred, let's hope Terry is as good of a driver as he makes out.*

Terry asked Fred if he could tell him a secret.

'Sure, Terry.'

'Well, Fred, it's kinda embarrassing, and I can't let any of my Aussie music purists know this ... if I did, I wouldn't hear the bloody end of it! But, well, it's a long drive, and I have the latest Billy Joel tape *The Stranger* with me. I've been dying to hear it again. Would you like to listen to it?'

'Sure, Terry, but why's that so embarrassing?' Fred asked.

'I dunno, guess it's just one of those things when you like something different to everyone else.'

Fred assured Terry, 'Hey, it's your truck, you play whatever you want.'

As the Richard Clapton's song ended, Terry asked Fred to pass over the bag from behind the seat.

Fred looked back for the bag; he could see one with two tiedown-type brass buckles keeping the main compartment closed, and there was a peace symbol drawn in fat black texter on the top flap.

'It's in the left-side pouch,' directed Terry.

Fred pulled the tape out and handed it to Terry.

'Have you heard much of this guy?' asked Terry.

'No, Tez, I don't think so.'

'Ahh this guy is a treat, he's like the American answer to Britain's Elton John, only less glitz and flare. Apparently, this is a concept album meant to be about his love for the city of New York. He's a hard bastard that Billy Joel, I can hear it in his voice. You'll hear it too, aggression like he grew up on the street, ya know?'

After the Billy Joel cassette finished, Fred slept most of the way, or at least pretended to sleep while Terry sung and whistled the entire way to Brisbane. It felt like forever, and Fred was relieved to step off the truck and bid Terry farewell.

Fred got dropped off at Bowen Hills Park, which was right next the hospital. He had too much gear to lug with him, so he looked around for walkers-by and decided it was safe to leave his gear in a pile hidden behind and in between the thick roots of a Moreton Bay fig tree that sat back off the road.

He made his way to the hospital entrance and asked for directions to get to Pearl's room, and when he arrived at her room and saw her laying in the bed, he said, 'Mum what happened?'

But he only got there just in time before his mother's last breath.

She managed to tell him, 'You did well, my son, I'm proud of the man you've grown to be.' She seemed so weak to look at, but the strength in her arms as she hugged him reminded him how strong a woman she was.

And just like that, she was gone.

Beryl and Fred sat close, holding each other's hands, neither of them wanting to break the silence.

'The doctor said it was some kind of metastatic cancer,' Beryl finally told Fred.

'Why didn't anyone tell me earlier?' Fred wiped some tears from his eyes.

'What were we to say, not knowing exactly what it was? And Mum didn't want to worry you. It all just happened so fast. Will you stay home, Fred?' Beryl's eyes implored him.

'Yep. I'm not going back up there; those bastards think they can treat people however they like.' And he lent down to hug his sister tight.

A week later, a Military Police vehicle arrived at the motel. The MPs confronted Beryl at the door, asking where Fred was. They then took Fred and put him in jail at the defence base in Holsworthy, until his hearing date.

He was ordered to remain in the cell for one week for every day he was AWOL: seven weeks. During that time, he put in his discharge, and it was dismissed –'dishonourable', they called it.

What a croak of shit, Fred thought. *After all I've done for the army and this country, this is how they decide to say thanks.*

On release, he was flown back to Brisbane, and his old mate Johno came to pick him up from the airport and take him back home to Harvestor.

Not a religious man by any means, he took to reading the bible he found in one of the motel rooms, in search of any answers he could find. *Weird stuff in here,* he reckoned.

He found a passage from proverbs and the feeling mirrored a similar anger he now shared towards the army: 'The roaring of God is that of a lion, those who provoke him forfeit their life.'

This rang true for Fred's view on his former employer.

The one who took him in, gave him a new home and became his new family. The one who transferred him from adolescent to the man he now was. The one that fulfilled his desires of exploration and adventure. The one that no longer existed, as if taken from him like the way suicide took someone you loved, without explanation and time to say goodbye.

He was alive, but was he living?

Fred had forgotten all that pleased him in life and started to wonder how he could dig himself out of his self-loathing trench.

Chapter Twenty-Two
THE MOGUL

Christopher Kace, a svengali character of a man, was born towards the end of World War II and grew up in the fifties in the Prahan suburb of Melbourne. But in the early 1980s, he moved to the affluent suburb of Hamilton in Brisbane. His father was a successful radio broadcaster, making a name for himself in the fifties and passing onto Chris the 'gift of the gab' qualities that came naturally to him.

The feel of a thick, well-greased wallet was important to Chris, and with a thirst for wealth, he went into business with eyes wide open, looking at all options and opportunities that came his way. After graduating from an all-boys private school at Caulfield Grammar in Melbourne, he cut his teeth on the stock market as a broker, with remarkable success.

After that, using the connections he had in the media, he became a financial journalist. That was the perfect place for his brash, fearless features with hubris. Chris would obtain insider information that led him to make successful business decisions, which allowed his company to grow into one of the richest Australia would ever see of that era.

He managed to buy up large parcels of land before they even were listed on the market, with an 'ear to the ground' knowledge of up-and-coming deceased estates. Chris realised the newspapers always left an obituary, which he read every day, looking for signs of deceased landholders; it was a winning technique for him. His company plan was buying up all the cheap land when possible, and when cattle prices dipped on the livestock market, he would buy the skinny cattle at a steal and send them on trucks to the new blocks of land to feed and fatten up.

These large southeast and western Queensland rural blocks were also laden with tall timber, mostly hardwood that had been growing for decades after the bullock teams had finished snigging logs half a century earlier. Blackbutt, tallowwood, Queensland box, stringybark, spotted, and flooded gums were just some of the trees logged for their qualities and used by builders and carpenters. Old-time loggers and timber cutters would selectively clear the areas, so as to not cause too much damage to the bush.

However, Chris couldn't care less for the bush, not like the old-timers did; his only concern was what it produced for his bank account.

The smell of fresh soil was almost intoxicating to Chris, and after the loggers were done getting the hardwood, that was when he would order in the bulldozers. The dozers would move in and work for a week or two, and they'd put in a dam next to a creek or gully to hold water. They also raped the land of all shrubbery and anything that stood in the way of creating pastoral grasslands.

If Chris wasn't well known in an area of interest to him, he would do everything possible to make a connection. It was relatively quick for him to have locals across the country working the land for him, either as a jackaroo or the local timber cutters. His company, Sintex, had now grown to over two hundred staff, and with fingers in a multitude of pies, he had begun to look at another option: open-cut coal mining.

However, he knew this had to be done with a more clandestine approach, so he hired five prospectors to work for him and placed them in remote locations across the east coast of the country, in search of the black rock, with hopes to turn his million-dollar company into a billion-dollar one.

Sintex had already bought out timber properties around Harveston and its sights had been set on Fred's town for the past year. Quiet discussions commenced with Uncle Jack and a few other select local property owners, with the idea of hardwood timber landholders alongside cattle stations leasing out or selling off blocks to Sintex. Chris made moderate to large offers, depending on the block, offering in the initial conversations sums of money he referred to as 'the carrot'.

But before formal discussion could take place, he made sure the landholders signed legal papers, non-disclosures agreements, preventing the farmers from going to anyone else in the town to seek guidance or counsel.

One of Chris' prospectors, Cruickshank, had been frequently staying at A Fine Motel for the past few months and had even found what he believed to be a large deposit of coal in the back paddock of Uncle Jack's property. Cruickshank lived in Newmarket, Brisbane. He had been a geologist for over ten years and worked for other start-up mining companies around Mt Isa in North Queensland, and he knew the signs of certain rock formations and the types of soil variants to test and investigate when trying to locate a suitable site to mine coal.

Drill results from Cruickshank's work had arrived in the mail at Chris' mansion on Dickson Terrace in Hamilton. Chris' brown eyes beamed as he read the positive news. 'You little beauty,' he called out loud as he walked over to the fridge and pulled a champagne bottle out from it. He poured a glass, and the bubbles flowed over as he sipped it down before taking a swig straight from the bottle.

Chris then phoned his office to inform them to

'prepare the papers with Jack asap', as he couldn't risk losing this deal. This news would enable his company to go 'all guns blazing'.

The next morning, he held a meeting and told the board they were to begin formal land purchase agreements with Jack – this would pave the way for the largest open-cut mine in the southern hemisphere and would be located in one of the valley landscapes to the west of Harveston.

Uncle Jack never planned on 'selling out', but as he aged, the reality of younger generations not wanting or willing to carry on the family business of life on the land made him realise that he couldn't see too many options ahead that would work. So, the way he saw it, instead of waiting for his death from either old age, sickness, or an unexpected farming accident, he took the position of selling now, to control the finances of his family and disperse the funds as he saw fit.

Chapter Twenty-Three

THE SECOND SESSION

July 1981

When Fred got to his second appointment with Doctor Leibbrandt, he objected to picking up any magazines to read or try to make small talk with Holly. He did glimpse over at her to find she was looking back at him, but he wasn't in the mood to raise a smile; she was at the start of her day and seemed busy anyway.

Fred's ears were ringing a pitch that waved up and down in volume. The clock in the corner ticked closer to his appointment time and then went over it by five minutes before the doctor came out and asked for him.

They walked into her office and sat down.

The doctor then gave him a pen, a piece of paper and asked him to complete some questions.

Fred stared with blank eyes at the questionnaire.

'Don't think about the answers for long, just try and tick the box that sounds like you,' she told him.

He read the line at the top: *On a scale of 1–10, how would you feel about …* With the questions below, he ticked the boxes. Afterwards, skimming over his answers, he noticed they mostly landed towards one end of the scale: flat, numb, avoid, wound up, angry, and afraid, were just some of the descriptions he saw coming from the answers.

He passed it back to the doctor, and she looked over the answers.

'Thank you, Fred, now do you think we could discuss what happened when you went overseas?' She chose the word overseas instead of using the word 'war', because she could sense Fred had some trouble talking about it and wanted to ease into the topic.

Fred had been focused on a loose strand of carpet edging that ran along the wall. 'You know …' He took an inward breath that expanded his chest. 'In the army, we're taught about, well, a lot of things. One of them is attention to detail.' He exhaled slowly before continuing, 'And without it, you can get yourself or your mate beside you killed. It's too much for me to explain right now, sitting here, but as a general observation, that's not a priority in the civilian world.'

Doctor Leibbrandt waited to make sure Fred was finished speaking, then asked, 'How often does this bother you.'

'Oh, I don't know,' Fred replied, getting agitated with the question. 'It was just an observation; I try not to let it bother me, all right.'

Fred was being evasive, and so the doctor became more direct with her next question. 'Did someone do something in Vietnam that lacked attention to detail?'

Fred looked at her with a smile on his face; he wanted to laugh at such a question. How was he meant to answer that? Where would he start? Fred lent forward and buried his face in his palms, and after a minute, he stood up and went to the window and looked out at the city view. He then began to talk with a shaky voice. 'I can't tell you what happened over there … but I can tell you that most days were filled with not knowing whether you'd live through another patrol, and hearing your mate's screams, and even your enemies' screams, for that matter, echoing around the jungle. And I can tell you that you had to watch every single step you took, or in a split second you could end up looking like meat coming out of a mincer. And then there were times when a hot wind pushed the scent of rotting remains towards your camp and it …' Fred turned around from the window; his eyes had reddened. He hadn't raised his voice, but there was anger surrounding him as he explained, 'And I can't expect you to know what it's like to pull the trigger, and then hearing silence, with no return fire and no time to clear for bodies. And all you can think is: did I get him? Or did he jump into one of his burrows and play dead?'

The doctor tried to keep her composure, but she couldn't stop her eyebrows from rising, leading to three forehead creases appearing, and then she frowned slightly, but she kept silent to encourage him to keep sharing.

Fred turned back to the window and stood cross-armed. 'And I come home to a dying mother and a dying town, and now some vulture is trying to pick over the bones before it's had its last breath.' He kept his feet planted but turned his hips to face the doctor. 'Well, fuck them!'

Doctor Leibbrandt was fixed firm in her seat.

Fred hadn't noticed how long ago she put her notepad and pen on the coffee table, and that the page was blank. 'Fred,' she said, pausing to make sure she had his attention, 'thank you for sharing that with me. It must have been hard. So, let me start by saying that I don't think you've done anything wrong and shouldn't blame yourself for these things.' She took a deep breath. 'You should be proud of your achievements and vision for the town.'

Fred noticed that the doctor seemed to have lost her native accent. He eased back into his seat. 'Well, what do I do from here, Doc?'

The doctor bowed her head and lent forward slightly, saying, 'You have to work on yourself. It's great to want to fix the town, and you should do your best at that, but if you're broken, you need to mend.'

Fred thought he knew what she meant, but he figured he needed more time to understand it better.

Chapter Twenty-Four

WHO WAS THAT ON THE PHONE?

July 1981

Fred was still reflecting about his yowie dream, as well as trying to recall some of Holly's features from when he was sitting in the doctor's waiting room. It was 9 am when the phone rang, and he let out a sneeze, then answered, 'Welcome to A Fine Motel, here in the heart of Duungidjawu Country, home of the Yuggera people. How can I help you?' His stomach hadn't stopped churning since he ate Ming's Chinese dinner a couple of nights ago.

A young voice asked if he had availability in the second week of November.

Fred checked the calendar on the wall and noticed that it was fully vacant, but he waited a few seconds to give the impression they were busy, and then replied, 'Yes,

yes, we have a spare room free if you'd like to book it. Is it just one room you were after?'

The line went silent for a while before the young voice asked, 'Do you have a pool table, and is there a mini bar in each room?

Fred sneezed. 'There's a pool table at the pub, and yes, we have mini bars in each room.' There were no mini bars, so Fred wrote a note: *What a is mini bar? Find out and make.* He then asked the customer, 'How many people and nights do you require? And would you like to hear about our winery, cultural awareness rock pool, and fresh-water lake tours, where our guests can go on a guided tour of the local winery and significant Aboriginal landmarks to learn about the cultural importance of the area?'

The phone line cut out and went dead.

Fred's stomach was now grumbling loudly.

The phone rang again.

'Welcome to A Fine Motel, here in the heart of Duungidjawu Country, home of the Yuggera people …'

It was a different voice this time. Fred's mind, for some reason, jumped to the assumption that it was someone from Channel Nine asking about prices and details of the hotel. They asked questions relating to the room furniture brands and bedding, as well as the sheet thread count. Fred, clueless to the term 'thread count' and what it meant, replied, 'It's high, like the highest possible thread count.' He talked up the hotel while his heartbeat grew slightly louder and faster with every question, and he tried to hold back a sneeze.

The customer finally stopped asking him questions, and Fred nervously got to ask them one back, with a slight stutter, 'Wa … well … ah … whom will be requiring the room?' Instantly, he regretted his words and palmed his forehead with his left hand.

The female on the other end began to explain, 'This is for … Ra—'

The line went dead.

Fred released a tiny high-pitched fart, squeezed out excitedly as he whispered the name, *'Raaayyyyy!'* Then he frantically tried to check the phone line for a dial tone.

Beryl, who was sitting in her chair next to Fred, was intently watching the movements, or lack thereof, across the road. She then noticed a distinct smell wafting in her direction.

Fred became flustered and told Beryl, 'The phone's playing up, so can you watch the phone, and if anyone calls, get their name and number. I'll be back in five minutes.' He walked briskly, pigeon-toed, to the toilet and entered the small room. He then closed the door, feet facing the toilet. After undoing his pants, he completed the confirmatory arse wipe, checking to see if he followed through on the fart before turning around and sitting down, saying, 'Goddamn it, this bloody stomach of mine!'

Beryl heard Fred yell in the background, but she

ignored him and continued to stare out the window. She then noticed the white four-wheel drive that had been hanging around town for a while now. With suspicious eyes, she mumbled, 'Who are you, and what are you up to?'

A few moments later, the phone rang.

'Beryl! Get the phone,' yelled Fred from the toilet.

But Beryl missed answering it. She was so absorbed in staring through the window, she didn't even hear it ring.

Fred heard the phone ringing again and yelled out, 'Beryl, can you get that this time?'

No reply was called back.

The phone rang again.

'Beryl, get the bloody phone, will you!'

She finally answered the phone, without taking her eyes off the car, and then helped the caller with their questions. The woman on the other end asked Beryl about an on-site swimming pool, and instead of informing them about the lack of swimming pool, Beryl replied, 'Yeah, I think Fred is dropping the kids off at the pool now.'

Fred had been furiously wiping his arse for the last thirty seconds, as fast as he could so he could get to the phone before the potential customer hung up. He wiped so hard, he busted his finger through the toilet paper, which only annoyed him even further, and he rolled his eyes. 'You bastard!' He finally finished and flushed the toilet, then frantically washed his hands before running back to the motel reception desk. 'Who was that on the phone?'

Beryl, still looking out the window, gave no reply.

Fred repeated, 'Who was on the phone, Beryl?'

'Just someone asking questions,' Beryl replied.

'Well, what did they want?' asked Fred.

'Aye?' asked Beryl.

'What. Did. They. Want?'

'They were wanting to know about the faculties,' Beryl replied.

'The faculties …? What bloody faculties?' Fred persisted.

'Eh, the facilities,' said Beryl.

'And …?' Fred paused. The cricket was on in the background, and India hit a six. Fred muttered, 'Ahhhh, fuckit,' under his breath. 'Who was on the call?' he demanded.

'Some lady.' Beryl paused. 'Had a strange accent, something about if we had gold-plated cutlery … and she wanted to ask about the toilets … it was strange.'

Fred raised his eyes to the framed photo of the Queen in a wattle-coloured dress hanging on the wall above the reception desk. 'I heard you say to them I was at the pool. Was it an English accent?'

'Yes,' replied Beryl. 'I told them you were dropping the kids off at the pool.' She snickered. 'What does that "English" sound like?'

Fred was oblivious to the English commentator of the Ashes test match cricket game on the radio, and instead wondered if he could do an English accent. He decided to give it a shot, saying with Sean Connery's James Bond affectation, 'Did it sound like this? I'll have a ssshteak sshandwich with sshauce thankshs. Did it sound anything like that?' He realised he had used more of a Scottish accent, but aah, it was too late!

Beryl giggled. 'Yeah, maybe.'

Fred whispered, 'Shit! Charles and Di … The Commonwealth Games … The Queen! Fuck it, B. This means we definitely hav'ta get a pool now, for Chrissakes!

Chapter Twenty-Five
THE SPAGHETTI INCIDENT

July 1981

That afternoon, Fred was at the motel, tuning into the third session of the Ashes. The cricket cut to an ad while the batters had a break for drinks, and an *A Current Affair* promotion came on. It was talking about 'schoolies' approaching. An interview with the various kids that made up the schoolies' crowd showed a bunch of them – all with big sideburns – standing next to a canary-yellow Holden Torana, talking about heavy metal and smoking rollies.

Fred blinked nervously, thinking about the up-and-coming schoolies in a few months' time. Although the motel was five hundred kilometres from the nearest schoolies location, he was reminded of the phone call with the younger voice who hung up. He decided to talk to Beryl about it. 'What if those kids from the neighbouring town want to come and stay here because of the attractions of our freshwater lakes, or the winery down the road?'

Beryl ignored him and just asked, 'Fred, what's for dinner?'

'Tonight, we're having the famous spag bog, just the way Mum used to make it.'

'And the garlic bread?' Beryl asked.

Ignoring Beryl's last question, Fred decided he'd better go and get started on dinner, saying, 'Beryl, can you watch the phone?'

She just mumbled back, 'There better well be garlic bread.'

Fred put on his apron and started to gather the ingredients. When he was cutting through the first of two white onions, he started to cry from the fumes. His eyes began to water like a tap with a leaky seal, which reminded him that he needed to fix the bathroom shower in room five … and he needed a water delivery. He called to Beryl, asking her to phone Johno and order a load of water, but Beryl remained hush. So, he walked to the office, trying to peer through his weeping eyes to dial Johno's number, squinting to read from the binder.

Johno answered, 'G'day, this is Johno.'

Fred stumbled over his words, saying, 'Hey, Johno, we're going to, *sniff,* need a load of water, *sniff,* next week.'

Johno was immediately concerned for him and asked if he was okay.

Fred replied, 'Oh yeah, bloody onions have stung me good.'

'Ahh … the famous spag bog tonight then, is it?' asked Johno.

'Yeah, mate,' said Fred.

'Room for another seat at the table?' asked Johno

'Absolutely! Seven pm sharp,' Fred replied, with another sniff.

'See ya then,' said Johno.

Fred had prepared everything, with ten minutes free to cook the homemade pasta he had just spent one hour prepping earlier that morning, and at 6.50 pm – after double-checking the clock on the wall to be sure that it was in fact 6.50 pm – he placed the pasta in the water and stirred it clockwise four times. He watched it with intent, making sure none stuck together. He added a couple of pinches of salt to the water, then began to set the dinner table.

The clock inched closer to 7 pm, and he stirred the pasta anti-clockwise four times and then clockwise once, before quickly going to the toilet, washing his hands afterwards. While he was in the bathroom drying his hands, he heard the phone ring. His eyes opened wide with fright and horror, and he yelled to Beryl, realising that it could be a call from London.

In slow motion, he took off running down the hallway while yelling, 'I'll get it, I'll get it, fuck!' But as

Fred reached and grabbed the phone, he knocked the phone base onto the ground. When he put the phone to his ear, he just heard a dial tone. He muttered, 'Ahhh, goddamnit!' He then looked at the grandfather clock standing against the wall, and it read five past seven. He realised the pasta was still on the boil and, with what felt like gravity pulling him back, he tried to gather speed and eventually ran back down the hallway into the kitchen to find that the water had boiled over and burnt.

He frantically reached for the colander and poured the water and pasta into it. Steam burnt his wrists and covered his face. He then tasted the overcooked broken pasta and exclaimed, 'Well great! It's bloody ruined now, isn't it?'

At that moment, Johno arrived, apologising for his tardiness, and smacked a six-pack on the table. Then he started telling Fred about the interesting conversation he'd just had with Cruickshank in the car park outside.

Beryl wheeled in.

Fred was slumped over the sink and told everyone, 'It's ruined! Sorry, guys, looks like it's just a bog without the spag tonight.'

'Have we at least got garlic bread?' quizzed Beryl.

Johno started looking through the cupboard while talking to Fred, telling him that the prospector reckoned that he hadn't found anything yet, just some gold flakes he had in a jar. Johno was unable to find anything useful in the cupboard. He then went to the fridge to put his beer away and saw the leftover fried rice from last Sunday's Chinese takeaway. He told Fred that the shirt the prospector was wearing, 'seemed to be fastidiously clean for someone who was meant to be digging and panning for gold'. Johno looked at Beryl and asked, 'Ah, have you heard anything more about this Sintex mob? He then ripped out the leftover fried rice container from the fridge, and before anyone could get a word in, tossed it into the pan with the bolognaise.

There was silence for a few moments; everyone just stared at the pan.

Fred looked at Johno. 'What the hell, mate?'

'Ehhh … it'll be good … it was my reaction to replace the pasta with rice … carbs, ya know?' Johno replied.

They sat down for the meal, all eating it before Beryl broke the silence.

'Mum never trusted Sintex,' she said over the volume of the cricket, which was on in the lounge room.

Fred's ears were already pricked after what Beryl said, and so he also heard the announcement on the television, 'It appears we have a pitch invader.'

Johno heard it too and stood up.

Fred followed him into the lounge room to have a look at the spectacle. Security guards ran onto the pitch to try and catch the streaker. Fred and Johno laughed at them trying to tackle the naked guy who was wearing a yellow and gold boxing kangaroo flag as a cape.

'Protect ya goolies!' yelled Johno at the television.

Beryl wheeled into the lounge room just as it was all over.

The English commentators remarked, 'Well, I don't think that will help the Australians out of trouble in this test.'

With the excitement over, they walked back into the kitchen and sat down, Johno helping Beryl back to her place.

Fred asked Beryl, 'Why haven't you said anything before about Mum not trusting Sintex?'

Beryl observed her spoon before replying, 'Nobody ever asked me.' And without much pause, she commented, 'Ya know, I think I prefer this meal with the rice instead of pasta.'

Fred looked over at Beryl in horror, and his jaw dropped. He wanted to say something but was uncertain how to reply tactfully.

Beryl stared down at her spoon again, which had a clump of rice and peas mixed through with some mince. 'I think I like the peas in this meal; the bolognaise hides the "peaness" flavour.'

Fred and Johno caught each other's eyes, their cheeks full and almost bursting.

Fred murmured to Johno, 'Don't say anythi—'

Johno sprightly asked Beryl, 'You mean you usually don't like the "peaness" flavour in your mouth?'

The penny dropped, and Beryl realised her penis statement was unfortunate. She told Johno to, 'Sit on it and rotate.'

Johno changed the subject and openly asked, 'I wonder why your mum never said anything about Sintex?'

Fred shrugged his shoulder and just replied, 'Dunno'.

Beryl glanced at Johno and said firmly, 'Because she didn't like to speculate and hated rumours.'

Fred replied, 'Yeah, but rumours are one thing, and a company coming in to take over the town is another.'

Johno felt some sibling tension and tried to cut through. 'Well, I guess it's like the chicken and egg thing … what comes first, rumours or the truth? It would come down to from whose perspective, really.'

Fred kept his eyes on Johno. 'I don't think this is the same thing, mate.'

The next day, while Fred was on a call with Johno to confirm the water order he made last night, he saw a Torana pull up in front of the motel. 'It's a bit early in the year for it, but it sure sounds like we've already got some schoolies here, mate,' Fred told Johno.

Johno knew that thinking about these kids spooked Fred, so he steered Fred back to his original enquiry and told him that there was an issue with the water truck as of this morning.

Fred just said, 'Mate.' *Sneeze.* 'I need the water. Can you get it to me today or not?'

Johno replied, 'Yeah, mate, relax.'

Fred hung up the phone abruptly, although Johno hadn't finished his sentence, explaining the issue he had with the regular water truck.

Johno, however, realised the importance for Fred and got on with it. And he decided, for expedience, that he would use the 'shit truck' because the water truck had currently broken down and was out of action.

A few hours later, Fred was on the phone talking to a customer when he heard the truck beeping in reverse as it backed up to the water tank. After about ten minutes, he looked out the window to see the brown truck instead of the blue truck and investigated it. His heart beat loudly, and he was trying not to panic after seeing the brown truck pumping into the drinking water tank. But sweat pooled on the left side of Fred's brow. He yelled at Johno, 'What the hell do you think you're doing?'

Johno yelled back, 'Getting your water order filled, like you asked.'

'The truck, Johno!' yelled Fred. 'What's going on with the blue truck?'

Johno shouted, 'I tried to tell you that the blue one was broken down, but you hung up on me, so I made a judgement call, knowing the urgency—'

Fred cut him off short, peppering him with, 'Just make it quick, will ya, mate. I can't have the guests, or anyone for that matter, seeing your bloody brown shit truck pumping into the water tank. Has it even been cleaned between uses?'

Johno attempted to reassure Fred, letting him know, 'It's okay, mate, I just switched the tanks over.'

By this stage, Fred was walking back to the office and missed the last thing Johno said. He took his notepad out from the draw under the reception desk and started to try and describe his feelings, like the doctor had suggested, and he wrote the first thing that came to mind:

Mind over matter …

There are countless types of killers out there, some of them unseen to the human eye. The killer sleeps, it waits in silence, for its time to strike. The killer can take your breath away, choking you without hesitation. Unless you're the first to strike, the key is knowing when that time is and how to attack. In a world where the rules are kill or be killed, the mind can play tricks, and without the strength to acknowledge and know how to combat your weakness, your fate may well succumb to the wicked within.

Not knowing what to make of this piece of writing, and not entirely sure where it came from, he decided to analyse it later. He closed the book, putting it back in the desk draw, and then he set about fixing a loose cupboard door in one of the rooms.

Chapter Twenty-Six

YOU'RE ON, FRED!

July 1981

That night, Fred drifted into a deep sleep. He began to dream that he was backstage in a dressing room at the Channel Nine studios, and through the walls of the studio, he could hear the audience laughing. He looked at himself in the mirror, then down at his notes, his heartbeat gradually getting louder. A television was turned on in the upper corner of the room, broadcasting the *Don Lane Show*, and at that moment, Fred realised he was in the same building.

A man with a pointy nose carrying a folder walked into the room and announced, 'Five minutes, Fred.'

Fred looked at the clock on the wall, which resembled the one in Doctor Leibbrandt's office, and the ticking became louder, pulsing in time with his heartbeat.

Don Lane sat at his desk on stage and told the

audience a joke, and then 'Moonface' Bert Newton was seen coming out dressed as an American Indian, wearing a traditional feathered head-dress, when suddenly a cream pie was thrown in his face.

Fred looked back in the mirror and said, 'That was a bit harsh,' but even though his lips were moving, there was no sound.

The man with the folder walked back into the room and yelled, 'Thirty seconds, Fred,' but Fred only saw his lips moving in the mirror – still no words could be heard. He did, however, hear a high-pitch ringing in his ears, like a swarm of loud cicadas in the bush.

As he walked out of the room, he picked up his notes from the desk but dropped them. Then his vision turned fuzzy, failing to allow him to pick them back up in time. He felt he was swaying as he started his walk along the red velvet curtain behind the stage. He was aware of the smooth fabric rubbing against his face.

The curtain caller stopped in front of Fred and turned around to face him, holding a folder under his left arm. He counted down on his right-hand fingers, 'Five, four, three, two, one,' then he pointed at Fred, mouthing the words in slow motion with a low-pitch slurring, 'YOU'RE ON, FRED!'

The curtain rose, and Fred was hit by a bright light shining directly in his eyes. The ringing in his ears turned up to a higher pitch and increased decibels as he attempted to look past the blinding light, trying to focus on something else. He began to speak, but he failed to make a sound.

The camera operator looked to Don.

Don was looking at Fred.

The crowd started to mumble.

Fred eventually said the first thing that came into his mind, which could now be heard. 'Do you ever get the feeling when you're alone that someone could be watching right now, but you know that's not possible because, well, no one else is there. But you think, hang on, I'll check over my shoulder anyway, and then you smell this old set of socks and jocks laying on your bedroom floor and wonder if they're in need of a wash, or if they're good to go?' Fred's confidence started building, and the jokes now rolled out easily.

The crowd began with a nervous giggle at first, and then, as Fred hit his stride, they gave whole-body laughs at the jokes that followed.

Don laughed, and Bert began slapping his knee while he watched Fred's animated comedy routine. He pointed and did this 'big arm' gesture, with canned laughter playing in the background, doubling up on the audience laughter.

Don, Bert and the audience stood and clapped when Fred took a bow at the end.

Fred woke up in a pool of sweat in bed and said, 'I need to build a swimming pool!'

~

That Friday afternoon, Johno was in the shed behind his house building a spud gun, keen to show it off to Fred. He called over to Fred from the backyard and told him to come for a beer.

Without much enthusiasm, Fred looked at the white piece of poly pipe, but he posed the question, 'Okay, but what have we got here, mate?'

Johno grabbed a potato, put it into the end of the gun then hit the trigger, sending the potato flying into the air so high it flew out of sight.

Fred stared at Johno. 'Reckon that's made the boundary, mate. Hey, Johno, what are you going to do with that spud gun?'

Johno thought about the question but took it as a comment.

'Reckon you could build a pool for me?' Fred asked.

Johno looked at Fred, 'Yeah, I could give it a good crack.'

'Thanks to Beryl's phone blurt a couple days ago, I'll need to have it sooner rather than later,' Fred said. 'Could you get one sorted easy enough?'

'Um. Yeah. I'll have a think, mate. I already got an idea, reckon I can make it work,' said Johno.

'Righto, mate, thanks a lot. Maybe I could plant those palm trees around the pool instead of out the front … would be a bit more tropical, hey?' Fred replied.

Later in the early evening, Fred and Johno strolled to the pub. It was coming up to the rematch for the rugby league 'State of Origin' game where Queensland would play New South Wales. Regulations had been put into place a year earlier, which related to where a player first played an A-Grade match instead of which club they were currently playing for. Johno pondered, 'We're going to give those cockroaches a smashing again this year with King Wally and Artie leading the team.'

Fred remarked, 'Don't forget Choppy and Fatty. They won't know what hit 'em!'

They both nodded in agreement as they sipped their beers.

The publican's wife, Jeanie, walked past, and Johno asked her if Reg would be out of town this weekend – Johno wanted to borrow the digger to start on Fred's pool.

She winked at him and whispered, 'Yes, honey, he's away, so the mouse can come out to play.'

Fred overheard and sneezed, causing beer foam to be sprayed over the bar runner.

Johno told Jeanie he'd swing by the window Saturday morning and grab the keys at around 10 am.

Chapter Twenty-Seven
THE SWIMMING POOL

25 July 1981

It was finally the weekend, giving Johno time to help Fred with the pool they'd discussed. Johno walked down to the pub in his thongs and stubbie shorts, not wearing a shirt or hat because he was trying to get a tan for the coming summer. He was off to borrow the digger, unbeknownst to Reg while he was out of town. He could hear the music coming from the pub as he walked past the white-framed windows along the outside.

The introduction sax solo of 'Baker Street' by Gerry Rafferty blew as he ducked his head below to avoid being seen by the few patrons that arrived as soon as the pub was open and were already perched early on their bar stools inside. He stopped near the window closet to the bar, allowing Jeanie to pass the keys to the truck out to him. She was carefree of the fact and consequences if somebody saw them interact.

Johno grabbed the keys and swaggered along to the music down the outside wall, kicking his toe on a star picket that had been cut off at ground height. He winced and muffled, 'Fuckin' hell! What idiot puts a star picket there?' He then shuffled to the shed around the back, his left big toe dripping blood with every step, bleeding all over his thong. He jumped up in the truck's marine-blue cabin. The Mack was about ten years old, once used for logging, but now it was converted into a flatbed truck.

When Johno started it, he gave it a big 'rev' that blew thick black smoke towards the tin roof and filled the shed. There was already a digger loaded on it, so he put it in first gear and took off.

He drove it over to the motel, parking it behind where the pool site was. First, he rolled a smoke then unloaded the machinery down the ramp before starting to break the ground where he felt the best place for the pool would be, without any consultation with Fred.

On the same journey in the shit truck earlier that week, when he'd spotted that cagey prospector, Cruickshank, he'd been out bush-pumping a septic tank for the cattle farmer, Uncle Jack. When Johno was at Jack's, he realised the tank had a leak, rendering it no longer usable, and he alerted Jack. He informed him the whole thing would need to be replaced. Johno recommended his brother would be the best person to replace the old tank with a new one. He told Jack, 'Jock lives one town over and replaces septic tanks for a living. He can do this standing on his head.'

Johno took Jock out to the property the following day with a new tank.

Johno then asked Uncle Jack what he wanted to do regarding the disposal of the old tank, saying, 'I can take it off your hands if you don't have a use for it?'

'I have no need for it, so it's all yours, mate!' Uncle Jack had replied.

Johno told Jock to take the empty septic tank to the motel and drop it out back.

After Johno dug the hole for the tank, he returned the truck and digger to Reg's shed, then gave the keys back to Jeanie, with a sneaky pash through the pub window, before getting to work on the tank in the place Jock had dropped it. He gave it a clean with a rough bristled broom and borrowed the dishwashing liquid and bleach from Fred's kitchen and laundry. He then proceeded to cut it down to size with an oxy torch before placing it in the hole he had been digging over the weekend. *Fits perfect. Fred's gunna love this.*

Johno looked up at the sky and could see rain clouds forming to the south. He yelled out to Fred to come outside and have a look at the new pool. Fred had been inside the motel, trying to figure out how to get his taxes sorted, not really paying attention to Johno's antics outside.

He walked out with his coffee in hand and asked, 'Where did you find the material to make all this, mate?'

'I was out at Jack's the other day,' Johno told him. 'His septic tank had a hole in it and couldn't be used anymore. I knew I could mend it good enough to hold water for a pool.'

Fred spat out his coffee, spraying it into the air like fine brown mist, and the look on his face turned sour when he realised what Johno had just said. He sneezed twice then said, 'Say again?'

'The septic tank was just going to be thrown out,' Johno told him, 'so, I had Jock drop it over here.'

'I think there may be some kind of health and safety rules about using shit tanks for swimming pools, mate,' Fred argued.

'She'll be right ... nobody's going to know,' Johno assured him.

'Bloody well hope so, otherwise this place will get shut down,' grumbled Fred.

Johno gulped then confidently said, 'I'll get the same chemicals over here that they use at the wastewater plant. I'll finish it off by throwing some aluminium sulphate into the mix. Don't worry, mate.'

Chapter Twenty-Eight

THE FUNERAL

1 August 1981

Uncle Jack suddenly died the following week in a cattle-herding accident. He came off his horse going down a steep path into a creek and was crushed under the horse. Everyone in the town was taken by surprise. They were all shocked and saddened with the loss of Jack.

The funeral was a few days later, and the service commenced with the eulogy delivered by Bull.

Fred and Johno arrived just as Bull began to speak, but the church was already overflowing with people, so they stood outside the main entrance with many others who were unable to fit into the dainty weatherboard church. They stood quietly, listening to details of Jack's life, and learning things about him they hadn't heard before. After Bull spoke, the priest read a chapter from the bible. Fred knew Jack wasn't religious, and in his head, he questioned the validity of this part but kept quiet to not let onto anyone what he was thinking. The service concluded, and the six pallbearers assembled around the coffin, then lifted it in unison and began to walk in between the church pews.

From out of nowhere, a fast-playing guitar started playing on the tape player, 'Glory Bound Train' by Slim Dusty. Fred found it enormously amusing, as the song was totally out of place. He looked over at Johno with raised eyebrows.

Johno did his best to contain his laughter, but his cheeks bulged, and his eyes opened wider.

They both stared at their feet, thinking how inappropriate it was to be laughing at what must have been the wishes of Jack for this song to be played, but they also couldn't believe how unsuitable the music was, regardless of the sentiment of the song.

The coffin was loaded into the hearse, which moved slowly out in front of the other vehicles already lined up on the road by the church. Everyone was preparing to make Jack's final journey through town. The cars passed slowly through the main street, and all the shops' employees walked out onto the footpath to pay their respects.

On the way to the cemetery, Fred and Johno were three cars back from the front of the procession. When the hearse stopped in the middle of the ups-and-downs heading west out of town, they all came to a slow halt.

Both drivers and passengers all poked their heads out

of their windows, trying to get a look at the front to see what the big hold up was. Only a few cars at the front could see the blood-orange Holden Monaro, which had skidded down the middle of the road before veering off and landing to one side in a ditch. Steam was coming from the crushed-in dinted bonnet, pushed in like a V, but there was no driver or passengers in sight.

On its side lay a cow in the middle of the road. An esky was lying next to the car, and several brown tallies were smashed next to it.

From Fred's position in the procession, he could see what looked to be a tail across the centre of the road. Jessie was sitting in the back, and she copied him, looking out her window, her tongue drooping to the right. Fred hopped out of his car, and Jessie jumped out her window, her tail pointed high with a firm wag.

They walked briskly to the front of the hearse, allowing Fred to find a cow hit by a car, but it was still alive and moaning in pain. 'She's in calf,' he called out.

Jessie barked, as if to agree.

Realising the calf needed to come out now, otherwise it would surely die along with its mother, Fred launched in behind the cow and steadied himself with his right leg laying along the cow's back and sat on his left leg bent under in the shape of a V. He then reached up into the mother cow with his right arm, trying to grip onto a leg or tail of the calf.

Bull ran onto the scene of the crash, looked at the brand burnt into the cow's hindquarter and said, 'That's one of Percy's mob.'

Fred struggled, paying no attention to Bull, huffing, puffing, and straining to pull the calf out before it was too late. He gave a huge wrench, and the crowd drew around to cheer him on. Fred was starting to get fatigued when Bull cried out, 'You got this, Fred!' Fred pulled hard again, and the calf fell into his lap.

Bull and Johno both stared at each other, then at Fred, in awe, and they failed to put into words what they'd just witnessed.

By this stage, a huge crowd had gathered, as well as Percy.

Percy had a 308-rifle slung over his shoulder, and he spat on the ground before he said in a gravelly voice, 'Well, Fred, looks like you're the proud new father of this baby bull calf – take care of it … or as we say, *gauremia*.'

Fred looked at the calf and replied, 'Well, I think we'd better call it Jack, my son.'

Bull helped Fred get the calf up and lead it to its mother's udder to get the all-important first dose of colostrum milk.

The procession started to drive around the cow, continuing enroute to the cemetery. Fred smiled while looking at the calf. He walked off with Jessie and Johno, who helped him put the calf into the back of the station wagon, when a gunshot from Percy's rifle rang out in the background, making Jessie wince. Fred noticed his ears ringing at the same pitch.

Back at the wake, everyone was having a beer and telling stories of Uncle Jack's antics out bush. Like the time he was wrestling a water buffalo and landed on an ant's nest and was bitten on the balls and all he could do was hang on for dear life. Or the time at the end of year footy party, when he tried to jump over the campfire after downing a bottle of rum, using a burning plank as a launch pad, and when it broke, he fell face first into the glowing red coals. He would have ended up with third degree burns if Big Kevie hadn't reached in and quickly pulled him out from the flames. Or the time he was driving himself and the cousins back from footy when taking a short cut in the EH Holden. The car ended up sliding off the road, landing in the lantana bush out the back of the forestry, blowing a hole in the radiator, and Jack then had to push the car the last mile into town.

Fred and Johno sat and had a quiet beer with Bull in the corner.

Bull looked at Fred and asked, 'Fred, how did you know what to do?'

Fred replied, 'I didn't, mate, but I remembered seeing Dad deliver a calf a couple of times when I was a kid. I just looked at the situation and knew someone had to do something.' He paused. 'I figured if anyone was going to dirty up their clothes on a day like today, it may as well be me. Just ah … instinct, I guess.'

Johno chimed in and said, 'Almost as dirty as you were with the pie in the park incident, aye, Fred? Tell Bull about that!'

Bull just said to Fred, 'Well, mate, you sure-as-shit impressed the mob today, much *wagoi*; it means "spirit", mate.'

That evening, Fred was sitting on the front deck with Jessie, enjoying a cup of tea in his pyjamas after an eventful and exhausting day. He heard Jack making calf calls, trying to get settled among the hay bed Fred made for him in the shed out back. Beryl was watching Ray Martin on *A Current Affair*, sitting next to the fireplace.

Fred stood up and walked over to the edge of the veranda, looking out at the stars. Jessie lifted her head up from nestled between her front paws. Fred slipped on his thongs and walked out into the night. It was a cool winter night, so he was rugged up in his old army jumper. Walking out into the darkness, he looked up at the constellations in the sky, thinking, *the milky way is big tonight.*

He remembered the stories his mum and Uncle Jack both used to tell, allowing him to visualise the emu stretched across the night sky among the milky way. He reflected on how the stars looked like sparkling diamonds scattered across a black blanket, and that without the darkness, the beauty could never be seen above, or even around us. He concluded: *Darkness must play an important role in life in some way; a chance to pause, or for growth? A chance to re-charge and prepare for the next day? A chance to reflect. A chance to concentrate on what's in front without being distracted by bright light.* Fred looked up at the stars, knowing he wasn't going to figure it out that night, and he decided to go inside to sleep on it, to ready himself for tomorrow.

Rumours circulated over the next few days on Uncle Jack's discussions with Sintex and his plans on selling out before he died, but the truth came out in time. As it was written, Bull was the main beneficiary in Jack's will and estate plan, and he was then approached by Sintex to continue with the land sale as Jack had planned.

Bull, however, politely told them to, 'Get fucked,' and 'If there was any black rock in the ground out here, it will stay in the ground where it belongs.'

This caused a minor setback in the company's plans for the town to become part of a mining operation … with the real 'nail in the coffin' still to be implemented.

Chapter Twenty-Nine
THE THIRD SESSION

3 August 1981

Fred was in the state capital, Brisbane, at his third appointment with Doctor Leibbrandt when Beryl received delivery of the 'Big Nut'. She signed for the delivery of the obnoxiously sized pair of nuts, and the workers jumped on the roof and began to install the giant sack-like structure on top of the motel. When Jeanie was 'commissioned' to design it, she was the only point of contact with the delivery and tradies the entire time. The morning of delivery, Jeanie was onsite to oversee everything and to make sure it all went to plan.

Not long after, Mal, the taxidermist, arrived.

Johno, who was already standing out front watching the tradies install the nut, accepted delivery for the 'Big Snag'. He reasoned to Beryl, 'We may as well use the same workers to install the snag while they're here, don't you reckon?' He even offered to pay them, saying, 'I'll grab a couple of cartons to install it for Fred as well, okay, fellas? This will surprise Fred when he gets home from his doctor's appointment in the city.'

One of the workers asked Johno if he was sure it was going to work out, and Johno confidently replied, 'Yeah, mate, go with it, for sure. Fred's had this whole thing mapped out for ages.'

Meanwhile, Fred was in the city at the same café waiting for his appointment at his doctor's practice in Paddington. He was planning on discussing all his negative rumination; however, his head was trying to juggle thoughts about the best things he could say in passing to Holly before and after the session.

During his appointment, the doctor asked Fred, 'How is the journal writing going?'

Fred looked at the naked bookends on the shelf behind the doctor. 'I haven't made many entries as such, but I think it's helped. I've enjoyed writing down thoughts to get my emotions on paper instead of letting them build up inside.' The doctor looked pleased with his answer, so he continued, 'You told me there is part two of your life story?'

Doctor Leibbrandt closed her notebook sharply and placed it on the table beside her. 'Yes. I'll give you a snapshot because I don't want to waste too much time. After I escaped my captors, I had to live on the streets and beg for food. I never lived in a spot more than a week or two at a time, so I could dodge child abductors and slave traders. When I was sixteen, I heard rumours of a boat that took people to South-East Asia and then Australia. So, I met with a smuggler and gave him all the money I had come to save. Nobody told us the stories of boats that sank, so I was unaware of the risk. And I couldn't swim but knew that there was a better life outside of my home country. The boat ride was long, rough, and dangerous, so I was seasick most of the way. Some people were knocked from the boat when a big wave caught us by surprise, even a baby fell into the ocean and drowned, the deck hands scooping the lifeless body up with a fishing net like it was a lost child's doll—'

Fred had heard enough, so he interrupted her, 'Thank you, Doc, that's upsetting to hear, sorry you had to go through that.'

She looked at him and said, 'I may not know your trauma yet, but I can help you work past it, so that it stays in your past but not near the surface.'

For a moment, there was an uncomfortable silence.

Fred felt awkward, so he began to talk about the first thing that came to his mind. 'It's not so hard to read and listen at the same time,' he said. 'I was sitting at this coffee shop just before, and I was reading the book you gave me: *Catcher in the Rye*. Anyway, I was reading along, sipping my coffee while having breakfast, and these two guys sat down one table away. They were obviously tradies of some sort, chippies, or concreters, with the boots they had on. I was about halfway through the book when the main character, Holden, you know Holden, he was also at breakfast talking to these nuns at the bar … meanwhile, the tradie guys next to me started talking. They chatted about their sleep patterns and how important sleep is, and one of them complained that if he had a glass of wine at night, then it prevented him from going to sleep till later. He said that he had no idea why, and I almost spat out my coffee. The other guy listened as if he had nothing much to say but clearly didn't want to offend him by saying how bored he was with their conversation. Anyway, I was reading my book and these nuns were chatting to Holden at the bar about the book he was reading – Shakespeare's *Romeo and Juliet* – and how Holden didn't like both main characters, but he liked Mercutio. Mercutio was his preferred character because he was more entertaining. Well, I was still reading and sipping my coffee and just thinking: Did I really go to war for these chimps to be able to sit and talk about their sleep patterns? Then I felt shitty, cause really, I never went to war for them or anyone, but I did go for the government, really … I went to help the US with a battle against another country, and whether Australia got involved probably wouldn't have helped the outcome. Then I felt low for comparing myself to people who did fight for this country, ya know. Those guys in World War II. How dare I do that! Maybe I'm being too hard on myself. Maybe this is what life's meant to be – one boring conversation after another. Unless you're drinking. Conversations would almost always be better with booze involved. I'm more open to listening to bullshit and talking it, as well. So yeah, I'm liking reading the book you gave me. Thanks for the idea.'

'I'm so glad to hear, Fred. It's an interesting observation you make. And I too think you shouldn't be so hard on yourself.' She smiled briefly before saying, 'Well, I have good news for you.'

'Okay … what is it?'

'So, it's been studied for a long time, but just last year, the third edition of the DSM was released.'

'English, please, Doc.'

'Ahh yes, it's basically a manual for mental health conditions, and that has allowed me to diagnose you with what's called "post-traumatic stress disorder" or PTSD for short. You also have been going through an "adjustment disorder" with the enormous change from army life back into your new life. Now, the stress you've been under, for some time, has contributed towards your stomach issues, likely irritable bowel syndrome, so stay away from hot spicy foods that may aggravate this. So, what you've been going through is normal, all things considered, and it will just take time and effort, but things will improve. I like to think happiness exists on the other side of heartache.'

Fred pushed his index finger into the corner of his eye and scratched it lightly, trying to comprehend what she had explained. 'Okay … um, yeah, thanks. I think.'

'Sure, and we'll discuss this more during your next session. In the meantime, keep reading, writing, and take this booklet on PTSD.' She handed Fred a wad of information. 'Wait here for five minutes until I get your scripts for your medication.'

Fred hadn't time to process what the doctor had just told him, but he was happy that she obviously knew what she was talking about and felt like he was on the right track.

When Doctor Leibbrandt returned, she handed the scripts to Fred and asked, 'Fred, when did you last visit your parents?'

Fred looked up at her from his seat, brows furrowed. 'Uh … I haven't been to the gravesite since Mum's funeral.'

'Okay, well …' Doctor Leibbrandt took a second. 'I think It might be helpful for you to visit it and let your parents know everything you're dealing with and what you're doing for them.'

Fred told her how he hated cemeteries.

'Life is about putting yourself in areas outside of your comfort zone. If you do this, you may find some closure, and don't be afraid of doing something that seems awkward or uncomfortable.'

Fred stood up and said, 'Righto, Doc, I'll see how I go.' He left the room and walked up the hallway to the reception desk.

When he paid for his session, he smiled widely at Holly.

She beamed back at him and asked, 'Did you decide to get the penthouse for the night, then?'

Fred shook his head. 'Nah, not this time. I've had too much going on at home with work lately, so I'll need to get back.' He then asked, 'Have you ever been out to the bush?'

'No, not really, but I'd like to one day,' she replied enthusiastically.

'Well, if you ever want to experience the wonders of the outback, give me a call.' Fred handed her a business card with A Fine Motel in bold print, the number and address below. 'That's me,' Fred remarked.

'Okay, I'll be sure to do that, thanks,' Holly replied.

As Fred turned around to leave, he heard, 'Um, Fred, do you like Joni Mitchell?'

'Ahh … can't say I've heard of her,' he admitted to Holly.

'Well, she's this great folk singer, and … uh, I have this here if you'd like to borrow it?' She pulled a cassette tape from her desk draw and passed it to him; her fingernails were painted two-tone salmon and scarlet with a slight orange tinge.

Fred's heart quickened, and he felt maybe Holly was as interested in him as he was in her, but he wanted to play it cool. 'Thanks, Holly, can't wait … to hear it, I mean, see you next time.' He then left the office, with a little spring in his step.

When he jumped in the car, he sat the tape on the passenger seat and looked at Jessie. 'Reckon we made progress today, Jess.'

Jessie tilted her head to the left, and her tongue drooped out the same side.

As he made his way through the traffic lights, without adverting his eyes, he reached across and picked up the tape then pressed it into the tape player. He looked at the track name, 'A Case of You', and slowly a guitar strummed with the most angelic voice Fred had ever heard. The song had his full attention, and the skin on his neck and arms began to tighten with bumps, and his eyes swelled.

Suddenly, tears channelled down the sides of his face. He couldn't remember the last time, not even at his mother's funeral, that tears had formed so freely. He had still felt numb inside, with a never-ending hangover that the war had left him with.

He then realised it was four years since his mum's funeral.

Jessie whimpered; she looked at him with concern expressed in her eyes.

'Now that is the voice of an angel, don't you think, Jess?

Jessie stared out the window.

Fred's tears continued to fall. 'Bloody hell, what's happening to me? I'm a mess, girl.'

He made it past the lights and turned off the pothole-infested bitumen road, beginning to travel home along the dry and dusty road.

Finally, he felt happy with himself and thought how well the sessions were going with Doctor Leibbrandt, or who he now referred to as Doctor Lina. The last interaction with Holly was everlasting, leaving a smile on his face for almost the entire journey home.

Chapter Thirty

HOMECOMING

3–4 August 1981

As Fred drove along, he liked to view the landscape passing him by, noticing the changes that often occurred with either climate or construction. When they got to the top of the range, Fred pulled off the highway nearby a field to let Jessie out for a run, and for him to have a break from driving. They were over halfway home, and he liked this particular spot.

Fred lifted the bottom wire of the barbed fence, and Jessie ran under, then he grabbed the second wire from the bottom and pushed it down as he bent and lifted his leg through, and in one motion (holding his hat close to his chest) the rest of his body followed.

'Didn't get me that time,' he told Jessie, referring to the spiked wire fence known too well for ruining any shirt or pant it could hook. 'Off you go, girl!'

Jess took off running through the grass. It was taller than she was, but Jessie cut through the thin strands and flouring heads with her tail weaving back and forth, chasing a toad or cricket like a shark playing with its prey.

The grass seemed to be waving back at him as if to say 'hello'. Layered colours of lime green, lemon yellow, apricot, and orange flourished below the bushy maroon seedheads shaped like fat feathers curling off to one side, pointing towards the setting sun. It had been a warm day without a cloud in sight but was beginning to cool off as the westerly winds pushed a large cumulonimbus, which impeded the sun.

Fred looked at the light-yellowing-brown and green patchy hills in the foreground – sparse, without any trees or bush – which were overshadowed by the darkest greens and blues of the mountain range behind it. *If only I could paint. It would have to be an oil painting with a large canvas … I hear oils are difficult to use, but from what I know, they would be the only paint able to give the detail this landscape deserves.*

'Okay, girl,' he hollered, then gave a big whistle. 'Let's go home.'

Jessie ran back, meeting Fred at the same spot of fence where he was waiting with it lifted again. She wiggled under the wire like last time and then jumped into the car door left open, sitting on the seat, panting and eager to hear the engine start.

Fred started the car, and Jessie gave a bark as if to say, 'let's go'. He sat holding the steering wheel and looked down at her. 'You're looking a tad thirsty, girl.' He reached back to grab the bottle of water and her dish, but the dish wasn't in its place. 'Right, guess you're drinking out of this, then.' He removed his hat and placed it upside down in the middle of the bench seat and half-filled it with water.

As Fred drove off, Jessie began to lap it up, and when she was finished, Fred put the hat on top of his head to let the small amount of remaining water cool him down, wetting the front and back of his shirt. Jessie never asked the question, but he felt the need to give her an estimated time of arrival. 'Not long now … I'd say another forty minutes.'

They were now nearing home, and off in the distance, Fred noticed a new phallic formation on top of his motel. He blinked tightly, attempting to focus, trying to make sense of these new shapes that appeared to be on the roof of his motel.

Suddenly, flashbacks of conversations haunted him like pieces of a puzzle all coming together to formulate the vision in front of him. Conversations with Jeanie and then with Mal. He remembered zoning out at the time of the original conversation, with worry about what the Big

Idea was and if it was going to fail. He vaguely remembered nodding and agreeing to them both to build the 'Big Nut' and the 'Big Snag'.

His heart started to beat louder and slowly increased in speed. He took off his hat and patted his forehead with a handkerchief from his pocket, checking his pulse while trying to look at the second hand on his watch to count his heart beats per minute.

When he pulled up on the street in front of the motel, Johno and Beryl were waiting there by the gate and mailbox, admiring both spectacles.

Fred hopped out of his car, walked up and stood next to them.

Jessie followed and then sat and looked up at him, tongue hanging happily. Seeing that Fred was unable to speak, she let out a bark!

Fred, meanwhile, was still trying to make sense of what was in front of his eyes, which now felt like they were burning.

Johno asked, 'What's wrong, Fred, you look like you've seen a ghost.'

Fred stuttered, 'Uuhhh … the doc … said I have PMS or something.'

Beryl laughed.

'I thought only women got that?' Johno looked at Fred with some confusion.

Fred hiccupped and mini-vomited in his mouth, then

his eye curled back into his skull, and he blacked out, falling, hitting his head on the motel-shaped mailbox as he fell. He lay on the ground next to the garbage bin on the street, semi-conscious, seeing Johno's blurred face as he tried to wake him up.

'You all right, mate? Beryl, call the ambo, will ya, it must be the PMS again.'

'They'll take ages, Johno. Just put him back in his car and we'll take him.'

'Stay with us, mate, you'll been fine, you've got a nasty bump on your noggin', but eh, you'll be right, mate.'

Fred dreamily said, 'Johno, big … I have big nuts.'

Johno laughed and agreed with Fred. 'In fact, it looks like you've got a big sausage to go with them, mate.' And he chuckled again.

Fred fully blacked out.

Johno ran over to his truck, and Beryl waited with Fred. Johno then struggled at first but finally lifted Fred then Beryl into the truck, and they rushed Fred to hospital.

When Fred woke up, Johno and Beryl were in the hospital room waiting. Jessie wasn't allowed in but refused to stay home. The gardener at the hospital had to make a bed for her outside Fred's window to stop her sulking.

Fred asked Johno, 'What happened?'

'Well, you don't have PMS, ya bloody drongo, you've been out for a few days, mate,' Johno replied.

The television news was on in the top corner of the room, and in the background, they were reporting on the tiny town out bush with a 'competition for the best local snag and an *extra big serving of meat and potatoes*'.

Fred's ears pricked up, and he gingerly sat up in bed. 'What the hell?'

Johno said, 'Mate, ah we have reporters from the news, they are, um, they're out—'

'Outside what?' Fred raised his voice in surprise.

A reporter peered through the window and saw Fred awake, so he alerted the team, 'He's awake!'

The rest of the reporters rushed into Fred's hospital room to ask questions – the nurses couldn't hold them back.

The first reporter was quick with the question, 'How did you come up with the idea, Fred?'

Reporter two quickly interjected, 'What made you go with the snag and nuts, Fred?'

'Can you tell us a bit about yourself?' asked the first reporter.

Fred paused for some time.

The reporters looked at each other, as there was an awkward silence.

Fred realised he had finally got his moment in the sun and figured out he needed to capitalise on this opportunity. He said in a semi-sedated, slow drawl, 'I'll only talk to Ray Marrr-tonn', before closing his eyes and pretending to fall asleep.

Johno announced with a circus-ringleader style and flare, at full volume, 'Right, that's it then, guys and girls, you heard it here first. Step right back, and out you go. We'll only be speaking to Ray, that's right, the one and only Mr Ray. Bloody. Martin. So, call your bosses and get him on the next plane out of Sydney and up here quick-smart!' Johno ushered the reporters and camera crew along, clearing them out of the room into the hospital corridor.

One of the reporters sulked, 'Bloody Ray, why does he get all the good gigs?'

'Gotta be the hair, I reckon,' a camera man replied.

The next day, Ray Martin interviewed Fred for about an hour.

Afterwards, Fred pushed his palms into his face and eyes and said, 'Gee, Johno, that was intense.'

Johno smiled at Fred. 'Reckon we'll get the buggers flocking to town after that?'

Chapter Thirty-One

THE BRIS

August 1981

A few days later, and on the other side of the world just off the Spanish coast, the news broke of the wacky motel 'Down Under', and two especially important people watched the television in their lounge room on board Her Majesty's Yacht, *Britannia*.

It was a completely different lounge room compared to the average Australian room. For one thing, it was on a yacht, and 'lounge room' was an understated way to describe the decadence of the big drapes and fluffy rug on the floor, the decorative Carolean ceiling patterns and the gold trim around the furniture edges.

A well-behaved Labrador dog sat at the couple's feet as they sipped tea from fine bone China cups and saucers.

Their butler walked in and asked, 'Will there be anything else, sir?'

The man replied with a thick British accent, 'Shh, please, I'm trying to watch this.'

'Sorry, sir,' the butler replied.

Ray Martin was on the television, talking to a Mr Fred Fine about A Fine Motel and the town.

'What types of things are there for the guests to do around these parts, Fred?' Ray asked.

Fred replied, 'Well … We just put in a swimming pool, all ready for summer.' Fred knew he had the spotlight and continued, 'There is a beautiful wine trail and bush walks. Oh, and yowie sightings are well documented too. The rock pools are amazing, and the landscape is … the most beautiful in the world to set your eyes upon. You could buy all the diamonds that have been dug up from under the earth's soil, but none would hold a candle to those that make up our emu out here in the bush night sky.'

The refined couple on the yacht looked at each other and agreed that this town was the perfect place for them to visit and catch a glimpse of Australian bush culture.

The British man watched the television and then turned to the woman next to him and commented, 'Diana, my love, would you like to go yowie-spotting?'

She gave a half-suppressed laugh. 'Well, yes, I think that would be fun, Charles.'

'Those Australians really are a strange lot, aren't they darling,' replied Charles. He then expressed, 'I remember a few years ago being interviewed by the most peculiar fellow; he was called Molly ... I don't think I've been interviewed by anyone who cursed so much and was as nervous as he.'

Meanwhile, Holly and Doctor Leibbrandt were on their lunch break watching the news when they saw Fred appear on the television. They instantly recognised Fred before turning the volume up to tune in closely. They giggled as they watched on.

Holly asked Lina, 'What do you think about having a girl's weekend out at this place sometime?'

Lina looked over at Holly and said, 'Do you have a thing for Fred ...?'

Holly blushed and said, 'Oh no, I just think it would be fun.'

Lina, however, could see there was something between Holly and Fred and decided to follow up with some 'girl talk' with Holly after hours.

Ray finished the interview with, 'And I was talking to your lovely sister just before, and she said that apparently there's some mining company opening up in town?'

Fred furrowed his brow and replied, 'Oh yeah, that mob Sintex are snooping around, good story for *60 Minutes,* I reckon – big company stealing land and ruining cultural heritage ...'

Reg and Jeanie were at the pub when the interview aired, and they told everyone in the bar to be quiet as they watched.

When Fred began speaking about Sintex looking to buy all the land and ruin the cultural heritage, Ray was quick to reply that he would be keen to investigate that 'story' further and ensure that the town had a voice in the matter.

A loud cheer rang out through the bar.

Ray then turned away from Fred and looked down the barrel of the camera to sign off with, 'Well, folks, it certainly looks to be a fine place to come for a holiday. I know where I'll be staying tonight. I'd go so far as to say that this is a place fit for a king and queen. Until next time, good night, Australia.'

Bull, who was in the bar, was the first to speak after the end of the segment, breaking the silence. 'That bloody bastard has done it, hasn't he? Good on ya, Fred.'

Back at the motel, the phones began ringing off the hook, and they were now booked out for several months. Fred had to even employ the kid two doors over to be somewhat of a roustabout and help with the day-to-day chores. He'd also had Johno do some landscaping around the pool, to make it look more established and not just a tank in the ground. Bull had even agreed to help teach Fred how to do the 'welcome to country' for the new guests, 'Because, Fred, you don't need to be a black fella to do one.'

And the best news was that Cruickshank had finally left the town, and word was that Sintex had well and truly been told to 'fuck off', as per Bull's initial request to them.

One morning, when Fred was at the reception desk of the motel, he answered the phone and spoke to a customer who was looking to book for three nights over the weekend. When he asked what name to put the booking under, the customer replied, 'Holly.'

Fred paused as the penny dropped. 'Um, Holly, from Doctor Leibbrandt's office?'

'Yes, I saw you on the television,' Holly replied, 'and it seems to be an interesting place to visit.'

Fred gulped and then picked up a pen and wrote in the calendar 'Holly' with a smiley face next to it. Then he asked how she had been and if she would like an 'accompanied, sort-of-bush-tour guide' when she came out to stay.

To Fred's delight, Holly replied with unbridled enthusiasm, 'I'd love that very much.'

Over the coming weeks, there were odd occurrences on top of the motel's Big Snag. Johno noticed that the front end of the Big Snag started to develop an indented ring around the tip.

One day, Johno finally posed the question to Fred, 'Mate, um … this might seem out of left field, but you're not Jewish, are you?'

Fred looked at Johno, somewhat bewildered, but still, slightly amused. 'Ahh ha, yeah nah, mate. Why do you ask?'

'Because … it looks like you've been working on a new concept for the Big Snag.'

'Mate, enough with the riddles and codswallop,' Fred told him. 'Whatever it is, spit it out.'

Johno asked, 'Have you had a look at your "ol' fella" lately?'

Fred looked blankly at Johno's cheeky grin. He muttered to himself while walking outside to look back at the snag positioned high up on the motel's roof. Then he gasped. 'Some fucker's circumcised my snag!'

'Yeah, mate,' agreed Johno. 'I never knew there was a Rabbi Mohel in town, but they've done an all-right job.'

'I betcha it was those fucking Jerky Boys, aye?' Fred said.

'No idea,' Johno replied, 'but you've gotta admit, something was bound to happen.'

Chapter Thirty-Two

EDGE OF THE WORLD

October September 1981 …

The Jerky Boy's pranks continued over the following months, and Fred tried not to let them get to him, because along with Holly's visits, which became more frequent, he wanted to make sure his focus was on her and giving her quality time in his majestic country home surroundings.

Holly and Fred were spending a lot more time together, doing all the things out bush that Fred loved and enjoyed sharing with someone. She was captivated by the area and everything it had to offer.

Not long after, Fred ceased his trips to see the Doc Lina, but he still travelled to Brisbane as often as possible to meet up with Holly, and she loved showing him around the city and Brisbane's surrounds.

It didn't take long for them to fall in love, and when Fred asked Holly if she'd like to move out to the country with him, Holly was more than happy and looked forward to the adventure. She eventually joined him at the motel to work alongside Fred as co-manager.

Holly never asked for much change at all, and although the idea of having a pet bull weighing over a ton in the backyard took a bit to get used to, she soon warmed to the idea. She even planted fruit trees around the house, realising that roses would never get to bloom with Jack around, but she did ask for a new pool to be built, having found out where the original tank had come from.

Fred, of course, agreed – in the back of his mind, he already knew that Johno may have overstepped the boundaries a bit on that one.

One morning, Fred woke and figured that the time had come; he decided to visit his parents' gravesite (like Doc Lina advised) at the local cemetery on the outskirts of town.

While he stood in front of the two joined headstones, the sound of magpies chortling in the nearby scribbly gum trees matched the key of the cicadas speaking in harmony to one another in the summer heat.

He looked at the stone engraving – 'Here lies Pearl and Frank Fine – Together in life and for eternity' – and began to tell them about his intentions with Holly. 'Mum, Dad, I'm going to ask her to marry me. I know you would have loved her as much as I do … well, I think you would have. She's an amazing person with such a huge heart and loving soul and … I don't need to get into all details, but I just wanted to let you know that everything is good, and we're doing all right.' He softly sniffed then said, 'Well, I gotta go get to work, love you both. He turned and walked back to his car.

And as he sat in the driver's seat, he placed his hands in his face and cried, babbling like a baby. Finally, he let it all out. He cried for everything he'd been through since leaving home to join the army and since returning home, and the things he had managed to overcome, and he cried with realisation that the life he now lived was nothing like he ever could have imagined when he was young.

Once he felt empty of tears, he drove back to the motel and parked the car. He closed the car door with a thud and walked to the back storage shed, putting his key into the D-shackle locking the chain that held the doors secure. He continued inside and pulled down on the light cord before he opened the top draw of the silky oak duchess and removed a wooden box with dove-tail cornices and a shiny varnish that had faded on the edges and was flaking on the corners.

Opening the box, Fred picked up the small leather draw-string bag and opened it. He pulled out a petite ring, admiring the shine of the gold ring and sparkle of the diamond that sat in the centre crown proudly, and he put it in his blue corduroy trouser pocket. He closed the draw, pulled the cord to turn the light for the shed off, then locked it up and searched for Holly.

Finding her in one of the hotel rooms making the bed, Fred knew it was now or never, so he bent down on one knee and said, 'Holly, you are the light of my life, the sun of my day and moon of my night, would you do me the honour of marrying me?'

Holly was taken aback, but after a few seconds of silence, she gave an emphatic yes and threw her arms around Fred.

A few months later, they got married as summer ended, when the heat wasn't so harsh. Holly chose the northern hilltop lookout over the valley for the location, and they held a small service one Saturday afternoon. Johno was the best man, and he nearly caused an upset when the rings were called for; he left them in the glove box of his ute.

After the service, they all made their way back to the local community hall for a catered affair, where Arthur and Margaret made sure nobody went hungry. Upon reflection, Johno reckoned 'they had the best quiche Lorraine' he'd ever tasted.

The next winter, Holly fell pregnant, and they were both excited to find out it was to be a boy. Fred was slightly relieved with the news, for he was afraid of having a girl as the first child due to certain unknowns such as 'how the hell do you braid hair?' and 'who's going to protect her when I'm not around?' but he thought if they decided to have a second child, a girl would be more than fine.

One evening, while Fred stood on the back veranda and looked out towards the mountains in the north, he felt he was standing on the edge of a new world. The seventies had well and truly concluded, and the eighties were already upon him.

The war was over, and he acknowledged that he now needed to take the next stage of his life by the horns and embrace the future with open arms – but he also knew that he had two fists still firmly gripped, weary of things that might threaten what he loved, just like that bastard mining company Sintex, and not being sure if he had seen the last of them.

Ultimately, he realised that the things most important to him in life now, and which should only ever be of his concern, were his family and close friends he considered family; being true and honest in all he did; and to become a better person and leave things in a better condition than when he found them.

EPILOGUE

December 2023

Fred woke in his hospital bed to the rattling and clicking of crickets chirping on his bedside table. He reached over and picked up his phone and looked at the caller id on the screen. His vision was blurred, having yet to put on his glasses, but he could make out some of the letters. *Bloody Johno*, he thought.

He motioned his thumb to swipe the screen to answer the call and, in the process, dropped the phone onto the floor. However, he could hear Johno call out, 'Hello, Fred', and then repeat it. Fred replied as loud as he could, 'I've dropped the damn phone. Can you hear me, mate?'

Johno was sitting on a cane chair getting some morning sunlight in the front yard at his retirement village. It was so peaceful at that time of day in the village, which was a gated community, meaning that only resident cars could drive along the tiny street and only the caws of the resident magpies could be heard. He always had a loud voice, which was easily recognised from a distance, but as he aged, his hearing had worsened, so this only winded up the volume levels of his vocals in most situations. He held the phone to his face and called out to Fred, 'I can't hear you well, mate, speak up.'

Fred looked to the ceiling and yelled, 'What are you doing?'

There were two hallways around the wing that led to Fred's room in the corner; one hallway had a bland-white tiled floor that ended when it turned the corner and changed into a speckled carpet, which Fred thought was likened to artist Pro Hart crawling through his splattered paint for Dupont Stain master carpets.

A young male nurse, who was at the furthest end of the carpeted hallway, had just started delivering breakfast to the patients on the floor, and he heard Fred yelling. He stopped short, holding the bed table tray, and pricked his ears to try and hear something more confirmative before he became alarmed.

He was in front of Doris Potter's room; Doris loved male nurses.

From her bed, Doris called out, 'Mind your shoelace, love.'

Johno raised his voice again to bellow, 'Speak up, I think you're in a dead spot.'

Fred rolled his eyes and mumbled, 'I'm in a bloody hospital, ya drongo.' He then yelled back to Johno, 'You're killing me!'

His voice echoed up the hallway and caused the nurse to escalate his sense of urgency. Immediately dropping the breakfast tray onto the trolley, the nurse attempted to dash towards the sound. Ironically, his wax-coated black shoelace, which got caught between his feet, latched onto the corner of the meal trolley, sending the top tray of food flying and the trolley toppling over with a crash when it hit the floor. He then scrambled along the hallway towards the commotion in Fred's room.

Fred heard the crash and bang when the food trays hit the floor, along with a fumbling fall onto the hallway carpet.

The nurse arrived at his room and stopped in the doorway to assess the situation. 'Is everything okay, Mr Fine?'

'Yes, mate, just dropped the phone ...' Fred stopped speaking and tilted his head to listen, and then he heard the footsteps of a hard-healed shoe smack on the tiled hallway floor. *That's doesn't sound like a nurse,* he thought to himself, and then he grumbled out loud, 'I'll call you back, Johno,' just as the footsteps stopped short at his door.

'Hello, darling, how are you holding up?' asked Holly as she poked her head around the door.

Fred looked at her with one eyebrow raised. 'Oh hey, gorgeous, I'm good now …'

He then reached over to find the poem he'd been working on over the last month. Fred picked up the notepad and turned to the final draft, looked up at Holly and asked.

'Could you have a read of it and ask if Atticus would like it, please, love?'

As Fred passed the notebook to her, she gave him a kiss on his cheek and sat down in the bedside chair and read.

Dear Atticus,

I am still in the hospital.

> *The food has not improved since your visit!*

> *I trust you are having a fun time, whatever it is kids these days do at your age.*

> *I hope you enjoy this poem I wrote for you.*

A choice

My child, when you fail to speak when words should be spoken,

When you say you gave your all, knowing it's untrue.

When you refuse to accept your belief may be broken

Oh me! You know, you're refusing to alter your view.

When you see wrong doings, my child, and refuse retribution.

When your failures repeat without recognition,

Oh life! If you don't fight for what's right no matter the threat,

Or know your own strengths or when your match is met,

When you confuse someone's trust for weakness

And make hay from their faith with little regard.

If you cut corners when somethings hard knowing full well the cost,

It may well be my child, you've lost.

My child when you mistake pride for arrogance and realise the difference.

When the heart swells with love without a care of your appearance

When you're out of breath yet still find another

Oh life! If darkness closes in, steadfast you focus on the light within,

When you're confronted with adversity, and pull on your boots,

When you get knocked down, learn from defeat, instead of retreat.

Oh me! You can do anything you must truly commit.

What is in your reach, you grab for it to succeed,

What feels too hard you decide to meet with strength,

A great verse is what follows going to great length,

Know that the steps to heady heights best be taken one by one.

Righteousness may be hard to grasp but if you can get a grip my child,

you've won.

P.s Don't forget to dream!

Love always,

Grandad.

-Fin-

GLOSSARY

Song list

Page 158: 'Mellow Yellow', Donovan.

Page 173: 'Howzat', Sherbet.

Page 174: 'Deep Water', Richard Clapton.

Page 174: 'The Stranger', Billy Joel.

Page 210: 'Baker Street', Gerry Rafferty.

Page 215: 'Glory Bound Train', Slim Dusty.

Page 228: 'A Case of You', Joni Mitchell.

Poetry list

Page 66: Woof, R.L Prior

Page 154: Treble and Bass, By R.L Prior.

Page 155: If, By Rudy Kipling.

Page 252: A choice, By R.L Prior

Pearl's Christmas Plum Pudding Recipe

Page 99: Naomie (Nao) Kunde and Granny Cavanagh.

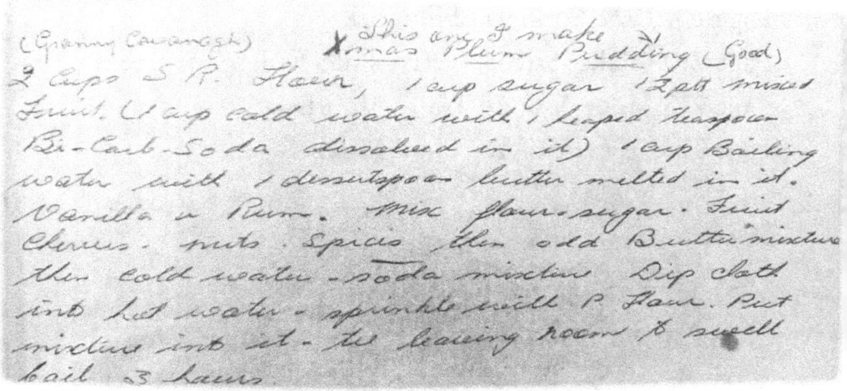

(Granny Cavanagh) This ony I make
Xmas Plum Pudding (Good)
2 Cups S.R. Flour, 1 cup sugar 1/2 pt mixed
Fruit. (1 cup cold water with 1 heaped teaspoon
Bi-Carb-Soda dissolved in it) 1 cup Boiling
water with 1 dessertspoon butter melted in it.
Vanilla & Rum. Mix flour, sugar. Fruit
Cherries. nuts. spices then add Butter mixture
then cold water-soda mixture Dip cloth
into hot water - sprinkle with P. Flour. Put
mixture into it - tie leaving room to swell
boil 3 hours.

1. 2 cups SR flour
2. 1 cup sugar
3. 12 pt. minced fruit, (1 cup cold water with heaped teaspoon Bi-Carb-Soda dissolved in it)
4. 1 cup boiling water with 1 dessert spoon butter melted in it.
5. Vanilla and Rum. Mix flour and sugar. Fruit cherries, nuts, spices then add butter mixture then cold-water soda mixture.
6. Dip cloth into hot water and sprinkle with plain flour. Put mixture into it.
7. Tie it up and leave the room. Let it slow boil for three hours.

ABOUT THE AUTHOR

Australians from the country often say they 'grew up in the bush', but few can claim they grew up living amongst it as Ross did. In 1988, Ross's parents bought 220 acres of scrub mountain, heavily laden with timber land. They cleared a patch at the peak to build a shed that would serve as their home until they could construct a proper house. Built by his father and mates without a spirit level in sight, the shed became their make-do home within a few months.

Surrounding their bush shed lay steep, undulating land, which the family transformed into a banana farm over the years, making their living from it. The shed, lacking fly screens or protection from nature, often welcomed uninvited visitors – snakes, goannas, possums, bats, and birds.

Ross lived in the shed, unchanged, until he graduated from Kilcoy High School in 2000. He then embarked on the next chapter of his life in the Australian Defence Force, where he began writing poetry while deployed in the Middle East in 2004. Following his ADF career, he spent eight years in the Australian Music Industry, recording on two albums as a band member and performing while completing a Bachelor of Music in Jazz. He graduated in 2013 and released a solo jazz album titled '*Heavy Sheddin'* with original compositions in 2014.

Drawn to the bright lights of Brisbane since moving to the city in 2002, Ross frequently returns to the country. He draws heavily from his past encounters and experiences, combining stories that highlight the beauty of the bush, music, and adventure in his writing.

Don't Forget to Dream is Ross's first novel with more are in the pipeline.

rlprior.com.au

www.ingramcontent.com/pod-product-compliance
Lightning Source LLC
Chambersburg PA
CBHW071432200726
48294CB00002B/610